THE LIVING OCEAN

EARTH AT RISK

EARTH • AT • RISK

THE LIVING OCEAN

by Elizabeth Collins

Introduction by
Russell E. Train

Chairman of
the Board of Directors,
World Wildlife Fund and
The Conservation Foundation

CHELSEA HOUSE PUBLISHERS

new york   philadelphia

CHELSEA HOUSE PUBLISHERS

EDITORIAL DIRECTOR: Richard Rennert
EXECUTIVE MANAGING EDITOR: Karyn Gullen Browne
COPY CHIEF: Robin James
PICTURE EDITOR: Adrian G. Allen
ART DIRECTOR: Robert Mitchell
MANUFACTURING DIRECTOR: Gerald Levine

EARTH AT RISK
SENIOR EDITOR: Jake Goldberg

Staff for *The Living Ocean*
EDITORIAL ASSISTANT: Mary B. Sisson
PICTURE RESEARCHER: Villette Harris
SENIOR DESIGNER: Marjorie Zaum
COVER ILLUSTRATION: Yemi

3 5 7 9 8 6 4 2

Library of Congress Cataloging-in-Publication Data
Collins, Elizabeth.
  The living ocean/Elizabeth Collins; introduction by Russell
  E. Train.
    p. cm.—(Earth at risk)
  Includes bibliographical references and index.
  ISBN 0-7910-1586-6.
        0-7910-1611-0 (pbk.)
    1. Ocean—Juvenile literature. 2. Marine ecology—Juvenile
literature. [1. Ocean 2. Marine ecology. 3. Ecology] I. Title.
II. Series.   93-26205
GC21.5.C65 1994   CIP
333.91'64—dc20   AC
        574.5

C O N T E N T S

INTRODUCTION

Russell E. Train

Administrator, Environmental Protection Agency, 1973 to 1977; Chairman of the Board of Directors, World Wildlife Fund and The Conservation Foundation

There is a growing realization that human activities increasingly are threatening the health of the natural systems that make life possible on this planet. Humankind has the power to alter nature fundamentally, perhaps irreversibly.

This stark reality was dramatized in January 1989 when *Time* magazine named Earth the "Planet of the Year." In the same year, the Exxon *Valdez* disaster sparked public concern over the effects of human activity on vulnerable ecosystems when a thick blanket of crude oil coated the shores and wildlife of Prince William Sound in Alaska. And, no doubt, the 20th anniversary celebration of Earth Day in April 1990 renewed broad public interest in environmental issues still further. It is no accident then that many people are calling the years between 1990 and 2000 the "Decade of the Environment."

And this is not merely a case of media hype, for the 1990s will truly be a time when the people of the planet Earth learn the meaning of the phrase "everything is connected to everything else" in the natural and man-made systems that sustain our lives. This will be a period when more people will understand that burning a tree in Amazonia adversely affects the global atmosphere just as much as the exhaust from the cars that fill our streets and expressways.

Central to our understanding of environmental issues is the need to recognize the complexity of the problems we face and the relationships between environmental and other needs in our society. Global warming provides an instructive example. Controlling emissions of carbon dioxide, the principal greenhouse gas, will involve efforts to reduce the use of fossil fuels to generate electricity. Such a reduction will include energy conservation and the promotion of alternative energy sources, such as nuclear and solar power.

The automobile contributes significantly to the problem. We have the choice of switching to more energy-efficient autos and, in the longer run, of choosing alternative automotive power systems and relying more on mass transit. This will require different patterns of land use and development, patterns that are less transportation and energy intensive.

In agriculture, rice paddies and cattle are major sources of greenhouse gases. Recent experiments suggest that universally used nitrogen fertilizers may inhibit the ability of natural soil organisms to take up methane, thus contributing tremendously to the atmospheric loading of that gas—one of the major culprits in the global warming scenario.

As one explores the various parameters of today's pressing environmental challenges, it is possible to identify some areas where we have made some progress. We have taken important steps to control gross pollution over the past two decades. What I find particularly encouraging is the growing environmental consciousness and activism by today's youth. In many communities across the country, young people are working together to take their environmental awareness out of the classroom and apply it to everyday problems. Successful recycling and tree-planting projects have been launched as a result of these budding environmentalists who have committed themselves to a cleaner environment. Citizen action, activated by youthful enthusiasm, was largely responsible for the fast-food industry's switch from rainforest to domestic beef, for pledges from important companies in the tuna industry to use fishing techniques that would not harm dolphins, and for the recent announcement by the McDonald's Corporation to phase out polystyrene "clam shell" hamburger containers.

Despite these successes, much remains to be done if we are to make ours a truly healthy environment. Even a short list of persistent issues includes problems such as acid rain, ground-level ozone and smog, and airborne toxins; groundwater protection and nonpoint sources of pollution, such as runoff from farms and city streets; wetlands protection; hazardous waste dumps; and solid waste disposal, waste minimization, and recycling.

Similarly, there is an unfinished agenda in the natural resources area: effective implementation of newly adopted management plans for national forests; strengthening the wildlife refuge system; national park management, including addressing the growing pressure of development on lands surrounding the parks; implementation of the Endangered Species Act; wildlife trade problems, such as that involving elephant ivory; and ensuring adequate sustained funding for these efforts at all levels of government. All of these issues are before us today; most will continue in one form or another through the year 2000.

Each of these challenges to environmental quality and our health requires a response that recognizes the complex nature of the problem. Narrowly conceived solutions will not achieve lasting results. Often it seems that when we grab hold of one part of the environmental balloon, an unsightly and threatening bulge appears somewhere else.

The higher environmental issues arise on the national agenda, the more important it is that we are armed with the best possible knowledge of the economic costs of undertaking particular environmental programs and the costs associated with not undertaking them. Our society is not blessed with unlimited resources, and tough choices are going to have to be made. These should be informed choices.

All too often, environmental objectives are seen as at cross-purposes with other considerations vital to our society. Thus, environmental protection is often viewed as being in conflict with economic growth, with energy needs, with agricultural productions, and so on. The time has come when environmental considerations must be fully integrated into every nation's priorities.

One area that merits full legislative attention is energy efficiency. The United States is one of the least energy efficient of all the industrialized nations. Japan, for example, uses far less energy per unit of gross national product than the United States does. Of course, a country as large as the United States requires large amounts of energy for transportation. However, there is still a substantial amount of excess energy used, and this excess constitutes waste. More fuel-efficient autos and home heating systems would save millions of barrels of oil, or their equivalent, each year. And air pollutants, including greenhouse gases, could be significantly reduced by increased efficiency in industry.

I suspect that the environmental problem that comes closest to home for most of us is the problem of what to do with trash. All over the world, communities are wrestling with the problem of waste disposal. Landfill sites are rapidly filling to capacity. No one wants a trash and garbage dump near home. As William Ruckelshaus, former EPA administrator and now in the waste management business, puts it, "Everyone wants you to pick up the garbage and no one wants you to put it down!"

At the present time, solid waste programs emphasize the regulation of disposal, setting standards for landfills, and so forth. In the decade ahead, we must shift our emphasis from regulating waste disposal to an overall reduction in its volume. We must look at the entire waste stream, including product design and packaging. We must avoid creating waste in the first place. To the greatest extent possible, we should then recycle any waste that is produced. I believe that, while most of us enjoy our comfortable way of life and have no desire to change things, we also know in our hearts that our "disposable society" has allowed us to become pretty soft.

Land use is another domestic issue that might well attract legislative attention by the year 2000. All across the United States, communities are grappling with the problem of growth. All too often, growth imposes high costs on the environment—the pollution of aquifers; the destruction of wetlands; the crowding of shorelines; the loss of wildlife habitat; and the loss of those special places, such as a historic structure or area, that give a community a sense of identity. It is worth noting that growth is not only the product of economic development but of population movement. By the year 2010, for example, experts predict that 75% of all Americans will live within 50 miles of a coast.

It is important to keep in mind that we are all made vulnerable by environmental problems that cross international borders. Of course, the most critical global conservation problems are the destruction of tropical forests and the consequent loss of their biological capital. Some scientists have calculated extinction rates as high as 11 species per hour. All agree that the loss of species has never been greater than at the present time; not even the disappearance of the dinosaurs can compare to today's rate of extinction.

In addition to species extinctions, the loss of tropical forests may represent as much as 20% of the total carbon dioxide loadings to the atmosphere. Clearly, any international approach to the problem of global warming must include major efforts to stop the destruction of forests and to manage those that remain on a renewable basis. Debt for nature swaps, which the World Wildlife Fund has pioneered in Costa Rica, Ecuador, Madagascar, and the Philippines, provide a useful mechanism for promoting such conservation objectives.

Global environmental issues inevitably will become the principal focus in international relations. But the single overriding issue facing the world community today is how to achieve a sustainable balance between growing human populations and the earth's natural systems. If you travel as frequently as I do in the developing countries of Latin America, Africa, and Asia, it is hard to escape the reality that expanding human populations are seriously weakening the earth's resource base. Rampant deforestation, eroding soils, spreading deserts, loss of biological diversity, the destruction of fisheries, and polluted and degraded urban environments threaten to spread environmental impoverishment, particularly in the tropics, where human population growth is greatest.

It is important to recognize that environmental degradation and human poverty are closely linked. Impoverished people desperate for land on which to grow crops or graze cattle are destroying forests and overgrazing even more marginal land. These people become trapped in a vicious downward spiral. They have little choice but to continue to overexploit the weakened resources available to them. Continued abuse of these lands only diminishes their productivity. Throughout the developing world, alarming amounts of land rendered useless by over-grazing and poor agricultural practices have become virtual wastelands, yet human numbers continue to multiply in these areas.

From Bangladesh to Haiti, we are confronted with an increasing number of ecological basket cases. In the Philippines, a traditional focus of U.S. interest, environmental devastation is widespread as defores-tation, soil erosion, and the destruction of coral reefs and fisheries combine with the highest population growth rate in Southeast Asia.

Controlling human population growth is the key factor in the environmental equation. World population is expected to at least double to about 11 billion before leveling off. Most of this growth will occur in the poorest nations of the developing world. I would hope that the United States will once again become a strong advocate of international efforts to promote family planning. Bringing human populations into a sustainable balance with their natural resource base must be a vital objective of U.S. foreign policy.

Foreign economic assistance, the program of the Agency for International Development (AID), can become a potentially powerful tool for arresting environmental deterioration in developing countries. People who profess to care about global environmental problems—the loss of biological diversity, the destruction of tropical forests, the greenhouse effect, the impoverishment of the marine environment, and so on—should be strong supporters of foreign aid planning and the principles of sustainable development urged by the World Commission on Environment and Development, the "Brundtland Commission."

If sustainability is to be the underlying element of overseas assistance programs, so too must it be a guiding principle in people's practices at home. Too often we think of sustainable development only in terms of the resources of other countries. We have much that we can and should be doing to promote long-term sustainability in our own resource management. The conflict over our own rainforests, the old growth forests of the Pacific Northwest, illustrates this point.

The decade ahead will be a time of great activity on the environmental front, both globally and domestically. I sincerely believe we will be tested as we have been only in times of war and during the Great Depression. We must set goals for the year 2000 that will challenge both the American people and the world community.

Despite the complexities ahead, I remain an optimist. I am confident that if we collectively commit ourselves to a clean, healthy environment we can surpass the achievements of the 1980s and meet the serious challenges that face us in the coming decades. I hope that today's students will recognize their significant role in and responsibility for bringing about change and will rise to the occasion to improve the quality of our global environment.

*People are drawn to the ocean because of its sheer physical beauty.
But it is also vital in maintaining life on the earth.*

T H R O U G H   T H E
L O O K I N G   G L A S S

People used to sacrifice to ocean gods so that their fishing would be good and their ships would come home safely. For them, the ocean was alive. In later times, natural philosophers continued to see a specialness in water. They called it the universal element, unformed but ready to take form, alive with possibility, a "sensitive chaos." But for most people, the ocean is a quite ordinary mass of water, appreciated for its usefulness. It is a place to find food and to dump the mountains of trash that are such a headache on land. Its beaches are places to build resorts and giant water slides.

The way people look at the ocean, though, is changing. With self-contained underwater breathing devices and deep-sea research submersibles, human beings can now survive beneath the sea for short periods of time and explore its vastness. Crossing this boundary between air and water is like stepping with Alice through the looking glass. A fairy-tale wonderland lies on the other side. Here, tiny creatures churning in a bucketful of water provide food for whales. Sea turtles peer curiously into scuba divers' masks. Molten rock erupts onto the ocean bottom and hisses as it cools in the frigid water.

People have also acquired eyes in the sky. From the perspective of a satellite, the continents lie bathed in a swirl of ocean currents and gyrating winds. Pictures from this height show the vastness of the oceans as they have never been seen before.

We can see that the ocean is alive in a way ancient peoples may have sensed but could not explain. Some of this activity is biological—the sea is full of unusual species of plants and animals. The interaction of moving water and moving air currents creates our climate. The movement of the oceanic crust at the bottom of the sea makes the continents collide and separate.

Two characteristics of the ocean make its role in the earth's climate particularly important. The ocean absorbs large amounts of heat, which it transports around the world in currents. Northern Europe has a mild climate, for example, because the Gulf Stream flows past, carrying the warmth of the tropics. The ocean also absorbs certain gases, taking them out of circulation in the atmosphere and modulating their effects on the climate. The gases dissolve in the upper layers of the ocean and pass through the food chain to the ocean bottom.

The ocean's great influence on the earth's climate suggests that any alteration to the marine environment could have dangerous consequences. Yet the mark of human activity is everywhere. Deep-sea explorers report stoves, cars, and kitchen sinks in water as deep as 14,000 feet. Divers in city harbors find pools of highly poisonous materials on the sea bottom. In the open ocean, the surface is often littered with debris. Plastic pellets can be found on the beaches of remote, uninhabited islands.

"Ever since that magical moment when my eyes opened under the sea, I have been unable to see, think or live as I had done before." Jacques Cousteau's reverence for the ocean is shared by many deep-sea explorers and scuba divers, who are awed by the diversity of life they find in the seas.

Some of the most intriguing ocean creatures are the masses of tiny, single-celled plankton found in the upper layers of the ocean. Phytoplankton are single-celled green plants that convert solar energy into food. Consumed by other organisms, they are the primary producers of food for all the other creatures of the sea. Some plankton create light, or bioluminescence, at night when they are excited by movement. In 1835, Charles Darwin marveled at the way the plankton in the waters around the Galápagos Islands made the oceans "burn." Today, in the waters around the Galápagos, fish and sea lions still explode in a mass of sparkling light at night. Their bodies are too dark to see, but their outlines glow. As they move, they leave long flashing trails behind them as they excite the surrounding plankton.

Phytoplankton, in the process of photosynthesizing their food, also release a compound called dimethyl sulfide that passes into the atmosphere. There, the dimethyl sulfide molecules become cloud seeds on which water vapor con-denses. The clouds that form on these seeds shade out the sun and reduce the phytoplankton's rate of photosynthesis. The very process of synthesizing food therefore limits the growth of phytoplankton, and the clouds provide a cooling effect to the earth.

The view from inside a deep-sea submersible research vessel.
Such machines have made it possible to explore conditions on the
bottom of the sea.

Other studies show that plankton can reduce the
temperature of ocean waters. Where large numbers of plankton
congregate, the ocean water is darker and more turbid. As a
result, sunlight does not penetrate as deeply to warm the ocean.
The difference in temperature when plankton are in the water can
be as much as several degrees centigrade. No one knows how
this temperature drop affects ocean life or the climate.

Larger ocean creatures often show curiosity for human
visitors in their realm. In the open ocean, schools of fish can
bunch so tightly together that divers see only a mass of fish heads
flying toward them out of the blue. As this wall of fish heads
reaches the divers, the fish break ranks. They swirl madly in pairs
around the divers, up, down, and sideways. Then, at some silent

signal, they pass on, looking like a swirling tornado in the blue water.

Scuba divers and researchers in submersibles can observe only a tiny fraction of such ocean life. Because water is 800 times more dense than air, it exerts a great deal of pressure. At sea level, the weight of the air is measured as 1 atmosphere of pressure. At 132 feet below the surface of the ocean, the pressure has already reached 5 atmospheres. Even though special rigid suits allow explorers to venture down to 3,000 feet, the average depth of the ocean is 14,000 feet and its maximum depth is 7 miles. Most of the ocean can only be explored at a distance—by sonar, robot submersible, or remote camera.

One of the most important tools for exploring the ocean at a distance is sonar echo sounding. Scientists fire air guns towed below their research vessels and record how long the sound waves take to hit the ocean floor and bounce back to a streamer of hydrophones towed behind the ship. Scientists use data from a series of these soundings to draw a topographical map of the chasms, flat plains, and mountains over which they are passing.

Another tool is deep-sea drilling, a technique developed after World War II. By taking cores from the ocean floor, scientists have gathered key data for establishing the earth's geological history. Recent drilling, for example, shows that the oldest ocean sediments are 150 million years old.

Satellites are a revolutionary leap beyond ships as research platforms. Remote sensing of electromagnetic radiation is the best means of studying global climate cycles or assessing the regional and global affects of human activities. Currently, scientists can measure the shape of the ocean's surface, surface temperature, the wind speed near the surface, the extent of polar ice, and the distribution of surface chlorophyll in phytoplankton in this way.

Submersibles have been used over the last 30 years to take scientists under the sea and to carry cameras or other sensing devices. Though unmanned submersibles are vital research tools, few can stand the pressures in the deepest parts of the ocean.

HEAT

One of the most noticeable aspects of climate is heat, or the lack of it. Heat is formed as the sun's rays reach the earth's surface. The oceans and continents absorb sunlight and radiate this energy back into the atmosphere as infrared energy, or heat. If this radiation did not occur, heat would build up within the earth and the planet would have a climate like Venus, which is suffocated by heat from the sun and has no means of cooling off.

Most of the sun's rays fall in the tropics. As heat radiates off the land and ocean, the air is warmed and starts moving. Three factors determine how it moves. One is the air's density. Warm air is less dense than cool air and floats upward. The second factor has to do with differences in pressure. Hotter air has a higher pressure than cool air and moves into areas of low pressure. Because air to the north or south of the tropics is generally slightly colder, warmer air from the tropics pushes toward the poles.

The third factor is known as the Coriolis force, which causes the winds to turn rather than to continue in a straight line. This effect is caused by the rotation of the earth. One way to understand this force is to think of trying to draw a straight line across the surface of a record spinning on a turntable. The straight line will appear curved when the record is examined. Likewise, the rotation of the earth gives circulating air currents a curved path over the surface, forming huge spiraling vortices around centers of high and low pressure. Winds veer to the right in the Northern Hemisphere and to the left in the Southern Hemisphere.

As the winds move, they drive surface ocean currents. Massive climatic changes affecting several continents can be caused by these winds. The winds associated with a phenomenon called El Niño, for example, push huge masses of water from the western Pacific into the central Pacific. California fisheries are thought to benefit from the current, while the coasts of Peru and Ecuador are flooded and the fisheries there have been decimated.

Self-contained underwater breathing apparatus, or scuba, gear gives divers the freedom to explore shallow coral reefs rich in marine life.

Deep ocean currents are also driven by the unequal distribution of solar energy within the sea. This inequality results in surface water becoming denser, sinking, and starting to move. When ocean water becomes saltier, a larger mass of salt particles is dissolved in the same volume of water. This happens in the polar regions when ice is formed. Salt leaches out of the forming ice crystals, leaving the ice nearly fresh and the unfrozen water more salty. It can also happen in the tropics, where the sun's rays evaporate surface water, leaving the salt behind. Either way, the

A tropical depression, an area of low pressure that may evolve into a serious storm, begins to form near Bermuda. Winds and weather are created by the ocean's moisture and heat energy and are further modified by land masses.

water becomes more dense. If a layer of water with a high salt content lies on top of a less salty layer, the salty water will sink downward and through the water beneath it. Water is also slightly compressible. As it gets colder, its volume decreases slightly and it becomes denser. Cold salty water sinks farther than warm salty water.

THE OCEAN AS A DISSOLVER OF GASES

The second impact of the ocean on climate occurs because of the ocean's role as a sink for dissolved gases. Once carbon dioxide is dissolved in the upper layers of the ocean, for example, it is absorbed by photosynthesizing plankton and is eventually carried to the ocean bottom locked in the tissues of dead marine animals. Carbon dioxide is called a greenhouse gas because, in the atmosphere, it traps the heat being radiated off the surface of the earth. By holding this energy in the atmosphere, the gas increases the heat of the air and of the earth's surface. Therefore, increases in the absorption of carbon dioxide by phytoplankton can have a cooling effect on the climate.

Scientists and environmentalists are currently debating whether human activity, such as the burning of fossil fuels, is significantly increasing levels of carbon dioxide in the atmosphere and increasing the earth's temperature. What is sometimes forgotten is that 55 million years ago—and for much of geologic history—the earth was much warmer than it is now. Vast subtropical forests once grew near the Arctic. Only as the earth's temperature lowered did the ocean cool sufficiently to sustain the deep, cold ocean currents of today. The fossilized tree trunks

Prepared by NASA, this computer-generated image shows what the ocean floor would look like if the water were removed. The long, winding Mid-Atlantic Ridge is clearly visible in the middle of the Atlantic Ocean.

sticking up out of the frozen tundra are a reminder that no climate on earth, hot or cold, lasts forever.

After the earth cooled, it entered a period of glaciation. Many ideas have been put forth concerning why the ice ages began. Perhaps slow, cyclical changes in the earth's orbit and in the tilt and orientation of its rotational axis altered the intensity of the seasons. Maybe the deciding factor was the splitting of a single supercontinent into smaller landmasses, or a decrease in the amount of carbon dioxide released from sedimentary rocks.

An increase in the earth's temperature, therefore, would in some ways be a return to past conditions rather than something new. The difference lies in the current dominance of humans on earth. Melting ice caps would raise the level of the ocean and change climate patterns. More heat and moisture in the atmosphere would lead to more powerful storms and increased flooding of low-lying coastal areas. People would lose control over the environment within which their societies have been built.

If the oceans become much warmer, they may not be able to radiate all this heat back out into the atmosphere. Recent research conducted in the Pacific Ocean in an area that is currently hotter than any other part of the sea has revealed that these waters are no longer able to radiate as much heat into the atmosphere as they absorb. The greenhouse effect has won out over surface radiation, and the ocean cannot cool itself. In effect, the atmosphere is clamping a lid on the ocean.

Fortunately, large amounts of water vapor are brought to this part of the Pacific by air currents. The clouds that form shade the ocean because, like ice or snow, they are shiny and reflect sunlight back into the atmosphere before it reaches the surface.

The results of this research paint a sobering picture of what could happen to the rest of the ocean if it was heated to a similar temperature. In areas that are not blessed with large amounts of water vapor, the ocean would lose its self-regulating capacity.

In this photograph taken by astronauts aboard the space shuttle, the peninsula of Florida juts out into the ocean. A band of haze across the central portion of the state has been caused by marine aerosols.

chapter 2

THE EVER-CHANGING OCEANSCAPE

Terrestrial mountain peaks are a conquered frontier. So many climbers now rope and axe their way up the highest of these mountains—Mount Everest in the Himalayas—that expeditions have been organized just to carry out the trash scattered on the mountain slope. Because of recent technological developments, however, another mountain frontier is emerging for exploration. This is the ocean floor, which features more than 24,800 miles of mountains, many higher than Mount Everest.

The topography on the ocean floor matches the mountains in unparalleled grandeur. Oceanic chasms plunge deeper than the Grand Canyon. A steep, straight precipice in the Gulf of Mexico extends for 500 miles and drops 1 mile to the bottom in less than 2 miles of horizontal distance. Canyons cutting through the ocean's floor are thousands of miles long.

Because this dramatic topography covers 70% of the earth's surface, any interpretation of global geological processes must take into account the current state of knowledge about the ocean floor. For example, less than 30 years ago, improved maps of the ocean floor gave support to a theory of movement of the earth's crust—the theory of plate tectonics—that has revolutionized the study of geology. According to this theory, the earth's crust is divided into huge segments, or tectonic plates. These plates move at a constant but very slow rate, only a few centimeters a year, which is approximately twice the rate at which a fingernail grows. Still, over billions of years, this movement results in the formation of new mountain ranges and the opening of new oceans.

The oceans also contain 97% of one of the earth's most vital resources—water. The power of ocean currents in this huge liquid mass has long been recognized. Columbus rode such a current to the Americas, and Spanish sailors picking up cargoes there quickly learned how to catch currents to speed their journey home. More recently, ocean currents have been understood as vital transport mechanisms for water, heat, nutrients, and chemicals all around the world.

THE OCEAN FLOOR

What does the ocean bottom look like? Near the continents, the bottom is a sun-dappled extension of the shoreline that is covered with mud, sand, and pebbles washed from the shore. The Mississippi River alone dumps 750 million tons of the North American continent into the Gulf of Mexico each year. Some of these shelves are very narrow; but others, such as the 800-mile-wide shelf off Russia in the Arctic Ocean, create a huge, shallow skirt around the continent.

Farther from the continents lie the continental slopes, which drop steeply away from land. Because only a limited amount of light reaches the canyons and winding valleys of these slopes, few plants live there.

The true bottom of the ocean floor begins at the foot of the continental slope. Red clays and thick oozes cover this floor. The red clays are made up of minute particles of rock debris from the land as well as dust from outer space. The oozes contain billions of shells of tiny plants and animals that have drifted down from the upper layers of the ocean. Because these oozes eventually harden into rock, ooze deposits from ancient seas are commonly found on land. Some of these deposits are as much as 1,000 feet thick.

Both the ocean floor and the continents lie on tectonic plates that divide the earth's crust into huge, moving pieces. Because so much of the earth is covered by ocean, most tectonic activity occurs underwater instead of under land.

TECTONIC PLATES

Tectonic plates range in size from a few hundred to tens of millions of square kilometers. These plates, which are between 75 and 150 kilometers thick, float like rafts on the partially molten material beneath them. As they move, they separate from or collide with other plates, forging new ocean floor and destroying old. Because the plates are rigid, these changes—as well as the volcanoes and earthquakes that accompany them—usually occur at the edges of plates.

New ocean floor is created as plates separate from each other at the Mid-Ocean Ridge. Researchers have likened this ridge to the seam of a baseball, winding around the globe from

A Portuguese man-of-war floating on the ocean surface. A type of jellyfish, this creature has a large air bladder that helps it float in the upper regions of the ocean where it feeds.

the Arctic Ocean to the Atlantic Ocean, around Africa, Asia, and Australia, and across the Pacific Ocean to the west coast of North America. It is the longest geographical feature on earth.

As plates on either side of the ridge pull apart, fractures form along the top of the ridge. Through these fractures, molten rock from magma chambers under the ridge seeps up to the ridge face, where it solidifies or erupts onto the ocean floor to form new oceanic crust. This new crust is much younger than that under the continents and has a very different composition. As the rock cools, it contracts. The deepest abysses in the Atlantic occur where the crust is oldest.

The Mid-Ocean Ridge does not run in a continuous line around the globe. Instead, it is cut into sections by transform faults that occur when two separating plates slide past each other. From above, transform faults make the ridge look like a series of steps rather than a straight line. Other types of discontinuities result in bends, jogs, and gaps in the ridge.

One reason for these discontinuities is the different rates of evolution along the ridge. Some of the plates at the ridge are separating "rapidly" (2 to 6 inches per year), while others are pulling apart much more slowly (around 1 inch per year).

While new ocean floor is created at the Mid-Ocean Ridge, old ocean floor is destroyed at subduction zones, where two plates collide with and push against each other. Here, one of the plates is subducted, or pushed under, the other. As this occurs, some of the sedimentary layers on the plunging plate are scraped off the underlying rock, much as snow is skimmed off the road by a plow. These sediments pile up into mountains in front of the overriding plate, while the subduction zone itself becomes a deep oceanic trench. Some of these trenches are remarkably long, extending 2,000 miles along the ocean floor.

To determine where subduction zones lie, scientists look for volcanoes and earthquakes, the signs of geologic disruption. The Pacific coast of South America, for example, experiences numerous earthquakes, some near the coast and others as much as 700 kilometers inland, under the continent. Along this coast, the oceanic plate dives under the plate on which South America lies. The earthquakes occur because of the temperature difference between the cold oceanic plate and the hot molten rock into which it is sinking.

One dramatic way in which moving plates change the
face of the earth is by destroying and creating oceans. For
example, 600 million years ago, another ocean lay in the general
vicinity of today's Atlantic Ocean. New mountain ranges
enclosed this ocean over the next 200 million years, and it
eventually disappeared. Then, 200 million years ago, today's
ocean developed in the same area.

Even as recently as 7 million years ago, the oceans did
not look as they do today. At that time, the Mediterranean Sea
dried up, leaving a great, crooked trench in the earth's crust that
was 2,000 miles long. The sea was doomed as Africa collided first
with the Middle East and then with the southern tip of Spain.
Sealed at both ends, the Mediterranean probably evaporated in
less than a thousand years. All that remained was a layer of salt
one mile thick.

Then, about 5.3 million years ago, Morocco and Gibraltar
broke apart and the land shifted. The Atlantic flooded into the dry
Mediterranean basin over cliffs that are estimated to have been
10,000 feet high, or 50 times higher than Niagara Falls. In a
dramatic rebirth, the sea basin, fed by an estimated 40 cubic
miles of water per day, filled in less than a century.

At the eastern end of the Mediterranean, the Red Sea is
even now an ocean in the throes of creation. This long, narrow
body of water is growing as the spreading seafloor pushes Africa
and Asia apart. At the current rate of growth (half an inch a year),
the Red Sea could be as big as the Atlantic in 200 million years.

The formation and reformation of oceans leads scientists
to wonder whether the continents were ever joined together in a

single landmass. Even as long ago as the 16th century, scientists raised this issue because the east coast of the Americas and the west coast of Europe and Africa look as if they would fit together almost perfectly. A wealth of evidence has since come to light to support this hypothesis. Twentieth-century scientists have found similar types of rocks and glacial deposits as well as similar species of plant and animal fossils on many continents. Such similarities would be extremely unlikely unless the continents had been joined at one time.

According to some estimates, about 300 million years ago, the earth's landmasses were fused into a supercontinent. Due to the size of this landmass, the interior was a great distance from the buffering effects of the ocean on climate. As a result, summers in the interior were blisteringly hot and the winters frigid. These temperature extremes may have caused many land-based species to become extinct. Also, this environment may explain why reptiles, which adapt readily to hot, dry climates, replaced amphibians as the dominant vertebrate species on earth. About 200 million years ago, this supercontinent, called Pangaea, separated into the continents known today.

A collection of seashells, the calcium carbonate exoskeletons that protect a variety of soft-bodied creatures living in the shallow areas of the ocean.

The oceans contain approximately 5 billion tons of water. The basins that hold this water are not monstrous bathtubs, with all the water the same temperature and composition from top to bottom. The deeper waters are colder, darker, and saltier than the top layers and, as a result, support different types of life.

The division between warm and cold waters can be as sharp and distinct as a knife edge. Divers, for instance, have no trouble noticing the dividing line, or thermocline, between warm and cold water. Often the discontinuity looks like a shimmering line in the water, and moving through it is like being doused with a heavy shower of ice-cold water. The waters do not mix very much—a diver in cold water could stick a hand back up through the thermocline and the fingers would immediately feel warm.

The division between sunlit and dark ocean water is not as distinct as that between hot and cold water. Light is lost as it scatters off particles in the water or is absorbed by the water itself. Some light penetrates to a depth of 1,000 feet, though the oceans (depending on their closeness to the equator) are well lit only to about 200 feet.

Sunlight is composed of different wavelengths, or colors, which are absorbed one by one as the depth of the water increases. Red light, with the longest wavelength, is absorbed first, and blue light last. On land, the color of an object is the color of the light it reflects. A blue coat, for example, reflects blue light and absorbs the rest of the spectrum. In the ocean, however, many plants and animals do not show their true colors because these colors have been absorbed by the water. One of the common Caribbean sponges looks like a coal-black vase in the

natural light available at a depth of 50 feet. But when a diver
shines an underwater light on the sponge, it reflects red light
and glows a deep ruby red.

The sunlight hitting the upper layers of the ocean is the
reason why these waters are warm. Much more sunlight reaches
the tropics than the polar regions, so the tropical ocean is much
warmer than polar waters. This inequality sets the ocean and
atmosphere in motion. Heat, water, nutrients, and chemical
elements flow through these two fluid media in currents and
winds.

Weather changes are quickly evident in the atmosphere,
which has a small heat capacity and is well mixed and fast moving. The ocean is sluggish in comparison and can hold a great
deal of heat. Because of these differences in response times to
climate change, the ocean has been called the memory of the
atmosphere.

THE CYCLING OF WATER

Leonardo da Vinci once called water "the driver of
nature." Water nourishes and supports living matter by flowing
through it—for example, by coursing from the roots of a plant
to its leaves. Water also drives physical processes by flowing
through and around the earth in a variety of forms. It circulates as
a liquid and vapor between sea, land, and atmosphere. It flows as
a liquid in ocean currents and freezes solid in glaciers.

After evaporating from the sea, water vapor either circulates locally or moves into the general circulation of the
atmosphere. This larger circulation is one of the primary ways
water is moved across the face of the earth. Ten times more water

As this rugged section of coastline in Australia illustrates, the sea batters away at the continents and over time changes their shape.

vapor, for example, passes over the United States each year than drops as precipitation.

Water leaves the atmosphere as snow or rain. More water evaporates from the ocean than rains down on it, so the balance is restored by river flow. The world's rivers deliver back to the ocean the water that evaporated from it and rained on the land. This cycling of water is a mixed blessing for shoreline ecosystems, however, because the water is accompanied by the pollutants that are dumped into the rivers along their length.

Ocean currents move vast amounts of water around the globe. Surface currents are primarily driven by the wind. They flow over—and often in a different direction from—the deep ocean currents, which are driven by differences in temperature and salinity.

The trade winds in the middle latitudes, which are the most constant surface winds, blow from the northeast in the Northern Hemisphere and the southeast in the Southern Hemisphere. By blowing strongly across the sea, they form currents on the surface of the ocean. These currents, influenced by the Coriolis force, do not travel in a straight path. They wheel around the edges of the ocean basins in large circular patterns.

Some of these surface currents carry vast amounts of water. The Gulf Stream, for example, is 50 miles wide and 1,500 feet deep off the coast of Miami. Ships choose their routes to take advantage of the power of this current, although grabbing a free ride is not as easy as it might seem. The path of the current changes unpredictably, and the outside edge of the current is a confusing swirl of side eddies and vortices. Experienced ship captains tell stories of flying along on the Gulf Stream and passing ships that were laboring hard against the current without even realizing they were caught in it.

Another well-known surface current is the Humboldt Current off Peru and Chile. As winds blow this current offshore, the surface waters are swept seaward and replaced by upwellings from the deep ocean. These cold, mineral-rich waters support tens of millions of birds and billions of plankton, fish, and other organisms. However, when winds blow huge masses of warm water into the area during El Niño, most of the animals and birds starve. The last major El Niño occurred in 1982–83, and another is predicted for the near future.

Deep-sea currents are caused as sea water at the poles becomes colder and more saline and sinks. An average of four million tons of water sinks every second throughout the year. This denser water then moves northward from the Antarctic and southward from the Arctic toward the tropics. How deep the water sinks depends on its temperature and salinity. The Antarctic bottom water, as the coldest water is called, slides down the continental shelf and into the deepest pockets of the ocean floor. It can be traced across the equator and as far north as the Bahamas. The Antarctic intermediate water, however, is not as cold or as salty, because melting ice and precipitation add fresh water to it. It also sinks and spreads northward, but it forms a layer above the bottom water.

The North Atlantic bottom water is formed in the Labrador Sea and in the ocean between Spitsbergen and Greenland. This water is made even saltier by the addition of water from the Gulf Stream, which is itself salty due to evaporation in the tropics. The North Atlantic bottom water floods the deep Atlantic, curves around the southern tip of Africa, and joins the Antarctic bottom water.

The flow of bottom water is dramatic. As the water moves from the floor of one ocean basin to another, it rises up over the edge of the first basin and descends as an immense waterfall into the next. These waterfalls can carry an estimated five million cubic meters of water per second, and they drop farther than any waterfall on land. By comparison, the Amazon River dumps only 200,000 cubic meters of water per second into the Atlantic.

The enormous masses of water leaving the poles are replaced by currents in the upper layers flowing poleward on top of the colder, more saline currents.

GLACIERS

Eight times in the last million years, snow in the north polar regions has compacted into glaciers rather than melting. As the glaciers thickened, they moved south, reaching as far as central Europe and the midwestern United States.

The ocean is affected by these glacial cycles. As water is captured within or released from glaciers, the level of the sea falls or rises. One of the greatest concerns about the current warming trend, in fact, is that many countries' coastlines will be submerged by rising sea levels as the glaciers melt. These changes in sea level affect ocean life as well. Coral reefs that are stranded above water or submerged too deeply rapidly die.

Ocean currents also circulate differently during ice ages. The last time glaciers moved southward, the currents that form the North Atlantic bottom water were shut down. As the glaciers retreated, a series of events occurred that demonstrate the importance of the bottom waters in the global redistribution of heat.

After northern Europe and the northeastern section of North America had been gripped by the cold for some time, the glaciers melted and flooded the North Atlantic with fresh water. The fresh water reduced the salinity and density of those waters, so they did not sink at the usual rate, preventing the cyclic flow of currents from starting up again. Once the bottom waters began to flow again 1,000 years later, the cold spell ended just as abruptly as it had started. The cyclic flow of bottom water controlled glaciation by circulating heat energy throughout the globe.

THE CYCLING OF NUTRIENTS

The currents move nutrients around the earth. Food also moves vertically in the ocean, as nutrients float downward toward the bottom. Most marine life exists in the top layers of the sea. There, fueled by the energy of the sun, pastures of phytoplankton create more than 90% of the organic material on which all other sea life depends. These single-celled plants are eaten by small animals called zooplankton and by fish.

The "living soup" of plankton is the richest concentration of life in the sea. With each progressive step along the food chain—and deeper into the ocean—animals' bodies grow larger, but their actual numbers shrink. Because food is dispersed in the ocean's waters and thus is difficult to find and gather, only a small percentage of the food energy available at each link in the food chain passes to the next link. Thus, there are very few hammerhead sharks and whales compared to the numbers of plankton and small fish.

The middle layers of the ocean are cold and only partially lit. Here myriads of fish move up and down through the depths and feed on a varied diet, including one another. Many creatures rely on speed, or defense mechanisms such as the stinging cells of the jellyfish, to escape being eaten.

In the pitch-black ocean depths live many creatures that are seldom seen, such as giant squid that are 65 feet long. Some creatures from these depths have been discovered by chance. In 1976, for example, a 20-foot-long shark swallowed a U.S. Navy sea anchor off Hawaii. The shark was given the name Megamouth because the bioluminescent bacteria in its huge mouth glowed in the dark.

As fish are caught and eaten and as creatures die, a rain of organic debris falls to the ocean bottom, or benthic zone. On the bottom, many invertebrates live by filtering these particles from the water. Among these animals are descendants of some of the earliest multicelled creatures to exist on earth, such as glass sponges, sea lilies, and lamp shells. Other organisms, such as worms, burrow in the sediments to find food that has settled there.

The sifting of vast numbers of plankton and other creatures down into the bottom ooze is more than a source of food for benthic creatures. As the bodies sink, they carry with them the chemical substance that the animals used during life, such as nitrogen, phosphorus, and carbon. This loss makes the surface waters less fertile and explains why the richest marine life is found where cold waters well up to the surface. On a global scale, the cycling of nutrients within the ocean—particularly carbon—helps to regulate the climate.

THE CYCLING OF CARBON

Carbon is chiefly stored in the atmosphere as carbon dioxide, and in that form it traps heat energy radiated from the earth. Because human activities, such as the burning of fossil fuels, release carbon dioxide, levels of this gas are rising in the atmosphere. There is some evidence that global temperature is also rising, and many scientists claim that this rise is primarily due to the carbon dioxide produced by human activities. Just as glass

A chain of volcanoes break through the cloud tops in this photograph of the island nation of Java.

keeps a greenhouse warm and humid, increasing amounts of carbon dioxide could trap enough solar energy to drastically alter the earth's climate.

Carbon is transported through two kinds of cycles—biochemical and geochemical. The ocean's role in the biochemical cycle is currently in the limelight because marine plants and animals absorb a significant amount of the carbon dioxide that people are releasing into the atmosphere. By acting as a sink for this gas, the ocean lessens the effects of air pollution.

During photosynthesis, phytoplankton absorb, or fix, carbon dioxide that has dissolved in the seawater. These tiny marine plants fix as much carbon dioxide—approximately 40 billion tons a year—as all the vegetation on earth. In the process, they release oxygen back into the water, which zooplankton and fish breathe. And by eating the phytoplankton, these animals move the carbon further along the food chain and deeper into the ocean. When the carbon reaches the bottom sediments, it is either assimilated into sedimentary rocks or gradually wells back up to the surface as the deeper water warms. Either way, the carbon is taken out of circulation for long periods of time.

Other plants and animals also fix carbon. Tiny plants living in corals conduct photosynthesis, and the tiny animals that make up the coral, called coral polyps, build reefs from a form of carbon they absorb from the water.

Because the oceans are a sink for carbon dioxide, the effects of releasing large amounts of this gas into the atmosphere have been dampened. How much longer the oceans can continue this role, however, is unclear. No one knows how much more carbon dioxide the phytoplankton can absorb, or what would happen if ocean temperatures rose enough to kill a large percentage of the coral. Dead coral is bleached white in color, and large swaths of these ghostly coral graveyards are reported by scuba divers every year.

Scientists need better computer models to chart the movement of carbon—as well as that of water, heat, and other chemicals—between land, sea, and air. Current models are unable to handle the large number of variables that can affect this movement. Only with improved models will researchers be able to accurately predict the effects of future climatic change.

In its geochemical cycle, carbon is slowly released to the atmosphere and oceans from rocks. This degassing, as it is called, mostly occurs at subduction zones, where one tectonic plate slides under another. Most of these zones lie under the ocean, where the bottom is covered by sediments formed from shells and other debris that contain carbon. Older sediments harden into rock and, as the subducted plate plunges downward, sedimentary rocks carried with the plate are subjected to intense heating. The change in temperature results in the release of the carbon. Because coal and petroleum are formed from the compression of organic material, they contain large amounts of carbon. By burning these fuels, people short-circuit the natural geochemical cycle.

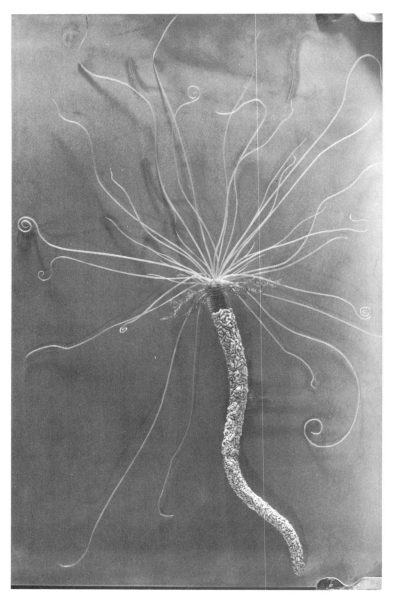

A tube worm of the type found near deep volcanic ridges, where new ocean plates are formed.

chapter 3

OCEAN ECOSYSTEMS

The ocean contains many different habitats. These varied environments support equally varied ecosystems of plants and animals that have adapted to living in them. Some fish in tidal areas can breathe air. Others have a mechanism that keeps them from freezing in subzero waters.

This panorama of life inspires wonder, but it also has practical implications for how people interact with the ocean. The different ecosystems are evidence of global physical processes, such as the creation of the ocean floor at the Mid-Ocean Ridge. Introducing change into ocean ecosystems, by killing off phytoplankton for example, can affect the global climate as well as the local web of creatures. This chapter discusses three types of ecosystems—the Antarctic environment, life in the deep ocean, and the shallow water ecosystem surrounding coral reefs.

ANTARCTIC WATERS

The Antarctic ocean is characterized by subzero temperatures, frequent ice cover, and a polar winter of continuous darkness. The ice cover has a tremendous effect on this ecosystem, as well as on the global climate. Ice has a high albedo, which means that it reflects most of the sunlight that hits it. As a result, the ocean does not receive the full benefit of sunlight even when it is present during the summer.

The season of light is very short at the pole, and fish and other creatures have adapted to take advantage of it. The water heats up only 2 degrees during the summer, so the very slightest increase in temperature leads to rapid bursts of growth and maturation.

These periods of biological growth start with the phyto-plankton. In the three to four months of continuous summer sunlight, they manufacture enough food to support all the life in the Antarctic seas. During the rest of the year, this energy passes through the food chain as predators consume prey and scaven-gers recycle the dead.

Large numbers of zooplankton feed on these phyto-plankton. The dominant zooplankton, called krill, swarm in thick clouds in the shallow upper layers of the ocean. Such a feast brings many animals to these waters, including whales, seals, fish, and birds. A single whale can consume a ton of krill in one day. Even explorers stranded on the ice have avoided starvation by learning how to catch these tiny shrimplike animals.

Farther down in the waters, most of the fish are members of just a few species. Two-thirds of the species and 90% of the individual fish belong to a group of perchlike fishes called the Notothenioidei. These fish are quite small, on average 6 to 12 inches long, with the largest reaching 4 feet.

The notothenioids dominate the Antarctic fish population because they are so well adapted to the conditions under which they live. Antarctic waters are very cold and dark, but many fish could survive such an environment. The notothenioids' trump card is that they are not bothered by sea ice. This ice, which covers the surface of the sea for at least 10 months a year, can easily penetrate fish gills and bodies. Once in the body, ice freezes body fluids and kills the fish.

Scientists have found an antifreeze molecule in the bodies of notothenioids. These molecules bind with ice crystals and prevent them from moving through the fish's skin and gills into the body. Even better, the notothenioids do not have to spend energy continually making these molecules. In other fish, small molecules such as these are filtered out of the blood by the kidneys and passed into the urine. In the notothenioids, the kidneys filter only selected molecules into the urine and the antifreeze molecules stay in circulation.

Most notothenioids live near the ocean bottom and lack a swim bladder, which is the gas-filled sac that helps fish float in

An elephant seal rests on a Mexican beach.

midwater. The evolution of some species, however, allows them to take advantage of the underpopulated midwaters of the Antarctic. The skulls and much of the skeletons of these notothenioids are made of cartilage, a substance that is lighter than bone. Their backbones are hollow, and they carry a lot of fat in their bodies, which makes them even lighter. As a result, these notothenioids can float in midwater without a swim bladder.

The bottom of the Antarctic ocean supports a densely populated and diverse community of animals. The water may be just above freezing, but it is rich in life-supporting oxygen. Glacial debris rains down from melting icebergs, and many animals use the gravel and stones in this debris as anchors to stabilize themselves in the mud.

Bottom-dwelling Antarctic animals grow slowly due to the limited food supply. A red starfish, for example, takes nine years to reach adult size. On the other hand, these animals also live much longer than their relatives in temperate waters, so their adult size is unusually large.

Some of these bottom animals serve as food for Antarctica's mammal population. A third of the diet of some seals is made up of invertebrates from the seafloor. Reaching the bottom does not seem to be a problem for these seals, which can dive as deep as 2,000 feet.

Antarctica's best-known bird, the penguin, also dives well. Its solid bones are much better suited to this activity than the hollow bones of flying birds. Also, the penguin's paddlelike flippers and streamlined body help it to "fly" underwater, and its densely packed, hairlike feathers and thick layer of fat protect it from the cold.

The success of the penguins in Antarctica can best be seen during breeding season. Hundreds of thousands breed together, trumpeting, braying, whining, and hissing at one another as they jostle for space. Adding to the noise are the hordes of chicks, which beg frantically for food from any adult returning from the hunt.

So many penguins nesting together could place great stress on the available food sources. Conflict is not too noticeable, though, because the two species of penguins found in Antarctica—the Adélie and the Emperor penguins—have developed patterns that allow them to live together in the same space. They raise their young in different areas, the start of their breeding seasons is staggered by as much as a month, and they hunt different populations of prey.

THE DEEP

Studying communities in water deeper than 300 to 400 feet is difficult. Scientists have resorted to dragging nets through the water and examining their contents, but this method is highly destructive and too random. Now, with improvements in submersibles, scientists can observe these communities firsthand. The animals they are finding are closely related to species in shallow water, but they show a wide range of adaptations to the peculiar environment of the deep.

The most noticeable of these adaptations is the ability to make light. About 90% of deep-sea creatures, from bacteria to fish, sparkle, flash, or glow with some form of light. Many of these lights are used to attract prey. Some squid have light organs at the end of their tentacles. Pelican eels sport a reddish light at the end

A penguin rookery on an island in the South Pacific.

of their tails. One species of anglerfish waves a glowing lure, while another has a forked light suspended from the roof of its mouth.

Finding mates is also hard in the dark depths. An animal must not only locate a mating partner but locate one when it is ready to mate. The deep-sea anglerfish has developed the ultimate answer to this problem. Once a male finds a female, which looks like a pear-shaped lump with an enormous mouth, he never leaves her. The smaller male attaches himself to the underside of the female's body and lives off her as a parasite.

Where no light is available, many creatures are blind. Where a little light penetrates, creatures have huge eyes or tubular eyes for binocular vision. Other senses can develop to take the place of sight. Grenadiers, relatives of the cod with a heavy head and long tail, can locate other animals by sensing vibrations when they move. They can also send signals to other grenadiers with their swim bladders.

The food drifting through these deep waters is not only hard to see but very diluted. As a result, deep-sea creatures tend to be more efficient and quicker eaters than their shallow water relatives. Pelican eels are 10 inches long, have huge, gulping mouths, and a brain case 1/4 inch long. Deep-sea starfish turn their stomachs inside out and digest food outside their bodies. They can also run along the ocean bottom on the tips of their arms at 100 feet per hour. In contrast, their shallow-water relatives drag themselves along at a mere 15 to 30 feet per hour.

The ocean floor itself is covered with a deep, loose ooze in which animals could easily sink. The sea cucumber, which looks like a monstrous caterpillar, disappears almost completely beneath the surface while hunting for small animals in the mud. To avoid suffocating, it absorbs oxygen through its tail, which it sticks straight up like a periscope. Other animals use stiltlike legs to walk over the ooze. Sea spiders have long, spindly legs that dwarf their bodies. In fact, their bodies are so small that some of the spiders' essential organs have ended up tucked into joints between their legs.

In the 1970s, scientists in the submersible *Alvin* were astounded to find animals living in what seemed to be a totally inhospitable environment—deep hydrothermal springs near the Mid-Ocean Ridge. Water spewing from these vents was known to be both hot and full of hydrogen sulfide, an extremely poisonous chemical. The animals, though, were obviously flourishing. They were huge—the mussels were a foot long, the worms close to six feet. And they were numerous. Only shallow, sunny waters with lots of photosynthesizing plankton were thought capable of supporting such flourishing communities.

The solution to the puzzle lies in the role of the sulfur bacteria. These bacteria are primary producers, able to manufacture their own food like the phytoplankton. Instead of relying on sunlight, though, they use hydrogen sulfide to fuel their synthesis of energy compounds such as carbohydrates. The energy in these compounds then passes through the rest of the community. Because chemosynthesis is the engine of life at these vents, these communities are independent of the food chain in the rest of the ocean.

The most numerous animals near the vents—tube worms, white clams, and mussels—have sharing, or symbiotic, relationships with the sulfur bacteria. The tube worm, for instance, is a closed sac without a digestive system or means of ingesting particles of food. At one end is a red gill-like plume where oxygen, carbon dioxide, and hydrogen sulfide are exchanged with seawater. The worm passes these compounds to sulfur bacteria living in one of its organs, called a trophosome, or feeding body. The bacteria make energy-rich carbon compounds, which the worm uses as food.

In the mussel, the bacteria live in the gills. Like the worm, the mussel has little ability to digest particles of food. Instead, it absorbs hydrogen sulfide through its feet, which extend into the vents. The sulfide is transported in the mussel's blood to its gills, where the bacteria oxidize it into carbon compounds.

Both the tube worm and the mussel have developed ways to carry hydrogen sulfide, a highly toxic chemical, through their

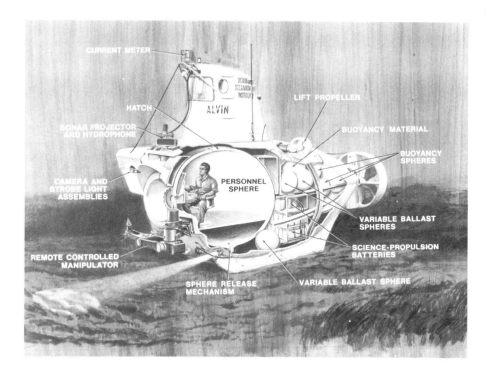

The submersible exploration vehicle ALVIN, which helped scientists locate the Titanic and other sunken vessels.

bodies to the bacteria. The worm's hemoglobin can carry oxygen and sulfide at the same time without letting the molecules interact. If the oxygen and hydrogen sulfide were to come together, they would form sulfuric acid, which would kill the worm.

CORAL REEFS

The upper layers of tropical oceans are extremely poor in nutrients, so the density and diversity of life growing on coral reefs is startling. Reef plants, however, produce enough food through photosynthesis to support the entire ecosystem. Because these nutrients are cycled and recycled through the reef system, reefs are not dependent on outside sources of food.

Reefs come in three shapes. Fringing reefs grow connected to a coast, or with only a narrow stretch of water in between. Barrier reefs also parallel a coast, but they lie farther from shore and are much larger. The best known is the Great Barrier Reef in Australia, which is 1,250 miles long and as wide as 90 miles. Atolls are coral islands that consist of a reef enclosing a central lagoon. They are formed when the top of an island volcano collapses. Hundreds of this type of reef dot the South Pacific.

Tiny coral polyps are the reef architects. These animals have a simple body structure: a main body cavity (or gut) where food is digested, topped with a ring of tentacles around a mouth-like opening. The tentacles contain stinging cells, which discharge an arrowlike barb and a toxin to stun microscopic crustaceans and other prey.

Most of the reef construction is done by hard corals. These corals create massive calcareous skeletons, which are the backbones of reefs. The polyps live in individual skeletal cups and extend their tentacles at night to feed. Part of the energy they get from food is spent depositing calcium carbonate on the reef at a rate of 12 to 24 tons an acre per year. When the polyps die, others grow on top of them. The living reef is only a thin veneer on a massive, ancient, dead structure.

Another intriguing aspect of the hard corals' life is their symbiosis with one-celled algae called zooxanthellae. These algae live in the guts of the coral polyps and build energy compounds through photosynthesis. The polyps receive a number

A starfish devours its prey.

of benefits from this arrangement. First, 95% to 98% of the energy compounds the algae produce pass to them. The polyps receive more nutriment this way than from the prey they eat. Second, the energy of photosynthesis allows the polyps to grow their calcium carbonate skeleton two to three times faster in sunlight than in the dark. Speed is essential, because the coral must build the reef faster than the strong, battering forces of the waves can break it down. Finally, the zooxanthellae use the materials, such as carbon dioxide, phosphates, and nitrates, that the polyps produce

A deep-sea anglerfish with appendages that emit light to attract prey.

as wastes. By recycling these wastes into usable compounds, the algae increase the efficiency of energy use on the reef. They also provide the corals with a means of waste disposal.

Corals' dependence on the algae limits where hard corals can grow. Because the algae need warm water, the corals grow through a band in the tropics. Algae need light, so few corals grow deeper than 200 feet. Deeper corals maximize their light-gathering capacity by growing into huge, flattened horizontal plates.

With so much attention given to corals, the importance of plants to the richness of reef life is easily forgotten. Many types of algae live on the reef besides the zooxanthellae. Some of these are primary producers that make energy compounds that are used by the rest of the reef community. Other algae recycle nutrients from the wastes of other reef creatures, and still others help form the physical structure of the reef by creating bits of calcium carbonate that add to the reef's mass or cement parts of it together.

Competition for space on the reef is intense. The competition starts with the reef builders themselves, the hundreds of species of hard corals, each seeking to extend its domain. Some species project filaments containing poisons into adjacent colonies. Others kill competing colonies by shading them from light. Soft corals, which are fleshy colonies without a skeleton, also join in the fight. They release chemicals that pass through the water and kill hard corals. Reef fish also kill patches of coral and eat the algae that grow in the dead spaces. They will fight other fish to protect these algae farms.

In light of this competition, the spawning habits of some corals are surprising. Corals can reproduce both asexually (such as by budding) and sexually. At least 100 species of hard corals on the Great Barrier Reef spawn in the same few nights in late spring or summer. Eggs and sperm are released en masse into the waters above the reefs, and the next day red slicks of eggs and developing embryos appear on the surface. The embryos grow

A group of individual coral polyps.

into larvae, which settle on the reef 4 to 10 days after the spawning night. There they develop into polyps. By budding, single polyps become coral colonies. New corals are visible to the naked eye at about 8 months of age.

The corals provide a massive, wave-resistant structure for a diverse and densely populated community of fish. Clown fish are particularly interesting members of this community. These small fish live among the waving, finger-thick tentacles of anemones. These tentacles contain stinging cells that paralyze other fish, which the anemone then pulls into its mouth. The clown fish, though, is not affected and rarely strays more than a few feet from its home.

Once a pair of mated clown fish claim an anemone, they are usually joined by one to six juveniles of the same species. As long as the adult pair is healthy and breeding, these juveniles do not grow much bigger. If, however, the male dies, the largest juvenile starts growing rapidly and matures into a male. All the rest of the juveniles grow a little bigger, and a tiny clown fish moves in to fill the bottom place in the hierarchy. If a female dies, the largest juvenile still matures quickly into a male. Then, the original male turns into a female. Several months later, the male-turned-female is laying eggs, and life among the anemone's tentacles is once again in balance.

Another tanker attempts to off-load oil from the Exxon Valdez, *which in 1989 spilled oil into Prince William Sound, Alaska, in one of the worst disasters for the marine environment in modern times.*

chapter   4

HUMAN   IMPACTS

The ocean suffers by its image. It is vast, so it is treated as an inexhaustible resource. It belongs to no one, so countries consider ocean resources as theirs for the taking. And, because the ocean is miles deep, it is treated as the ultimate dumping ground for wastes. Until recently, dumping wastes in the ocean was the choice of least resistance because no one lives there to protest.

This chapter examines two of the most significant impacts humans have on the ocean—the management of fisheries and the handling of wastes. Communities have long used the oceans as a source of food. In the last two centuries, technologies designed to improve the efficiency and profitability of commercial fishing have resulted in a worldwide threat to fish and marine mammal populations. The ocean has also long been used for dumping wastes, but the increased volume and toxicity of today's wastes threaten ocean ecologies and the health of people who utilize the ocean's resources.

International market demands and the pressures of growing populations lead to the mismanagement of fisheries. If market demand drives up the price of a fish product, fisheries attempt to reap the largest profit margin in the shortest period of time by using increasingly destructive fishing methods. The common practice of fishing with drift nets and purse-seine nets is an example of blatant destruction in pursuit of profit.

Every night, more than a thousand ships from Japan, Taiwan, and South Korea roll out close to 30,000 miles of drift nets across the seas. The nets are intended to catch tuna and squid, but these nets also snare 800,000 seabirds and up to 120,000 dolphins, whales, and seals each year. Another tactic of tuna boats is to spread baglike nets called purse seines around dolphins because tuna are known to swim below them. This technique kills at least 100,000 dolphins each year in the eastern tropical Pacific alone. To make matters worse, more than 600 miles of nets are lost or cut loose every year. These derelict nets, which are usually made of nondegradable plastic filament, continue to entangle and kill seabirds, marine mammals, and fish for decades.

Asian markets have encouraged another highly wasteful technique, called finning. Many sharks are caught in the process of hunting other species, such as swordfish, but shark meat can usually be sold for only 30¢ to 50¢ a pound. Shark fins, however, are worth $8 to $12.50 a pound in Asia, where they are used to make shark-fin soup. Responding to this demand, many fishermen intentionally hunt sharks. Since the sharks' fins are the only highly profitable part of their bodies, the fishermen cut them off and throw the maimed creatures overboard to die. Between intentional and unintentional catches, fisheries kill over 100 million sharks each year.

As coastal waters become barren because of overfishing, fishing fleets become larger and hunt farther out to sea. Once these new grounds are impoverished, the boats need even better technologies to reach still deeper waters. The fishermen are desperate to earn a living and to turn a quick profit to repay the loans on their boats and equipment. As a result, they plunder every available resource from the ocean and ignore the effect of this destruction on their future livelihood.

The response to decreasing fish stocks is often to attack other marine animals thought to be competing for these resources. In the 1950s, white beluga whales were slaughtered in the St. Lawrence River in Canada for this reason, even though the beluga population had already been cut in half by whalers wanting their blubber and oil. And in the 1970s, Japanese fishermen killed more than 6,000 dolphins in a misguided effort to protect local fish stocks. The decline in these stocks was not caused by the dolphins but was the result of climate changes, coastal pollution, and the overharvesting of fisheries by the fishermen themselves.

Overfishing never affects just the single species being hunted. Large numbers of all sorts of creatures, from crabs to whales, are killed as a side effect of fishing activities. The decline of a specific fish population throws shock waves up and down a food chain. Fish eaten by that species start to proliferate because they have lost a predator, and fish farther up the food chain are put under stress because they have lost a food source. Once the original species has become so scarce that harvesting it no longer

In the 1970s, Japanese fishermen slaughtered a large number of dolphins, believing that these creatures were consuming the fish they depended on for their livelihood.

provides a profit, the fish farther up the food chain are often the next target of the fishermen.

Some marine creatures rebound quickly once the pressure of fishing has been lifted. Others, such as sharks, are very slow to grow and mature. Shark embryos require as much as one or two years to develop before birth, and many sharks cannot reproduce until after reaching 12 to 15 years of age.

If breeding cycles were the primary limiting factor in the recovery of a declining fish or marine mammal population, most species would eventually return in sizeable numbers. Pollution, however, presents at least as grave a danger to ocean creatures as overfishing.

WASTE HANDLING

Wastes from every human activity eventually reach the ocean. Although the pathways by which wastes move to the ocean are easily identified, the resulting harm to ocean creatures and to human health has not yet been so well defined. Outbreaks of disease in people who eat seafood and the schools of dead fish washed up on beaches are obvious indicators of high pollution levels. However, scientists have not yet fully assessed the effects of smaller concentrations of pollutants moving throughout the web of marine life.

The primary ways by which pollutants enter the ocean are through pipelines from factories and waste-treatment plants, accidental and intentional spillage and dumping from ships at sea, the runoff of agricultural chemicals into rivers, and atmospheric precipitation.

Currently, more than 1,300 major industrial facilities in the United States use pipelines to discharge sewage into the ocean. These wastes often flow untreated into coastal waters and the mouths of rivers, or estuaries. Also, inland facilities pipe sewage into rivers, which then carry the contaminants to the ocean. Most of the metals and organic chemicals dumped into the ocean are contained in industrial sewage.

Human wastes are also often piped into the ocean as raw sewage. Sometimes even municipal sewage-treatment plants pass raw sewage into the ocean. Many of these plants are old and too small to handle current volumes of waste. In addition, most do not treat the toxic household fluids, such as paints, that people flush down sinks or the industrial materials that also come through this system.

Off the U.S. coast, barges carry a variety of wastes to established dumping sites. The largest volume of this material —about 180 million metric tons—is from dredging activities, such as deepening harbors. In the past, this dredged material has been relatively uncontaminated. Now, however, this material contains a wide range of pollutants that have settled to the bottom of harbors and waterways.

Wastes are also illegally dumped into coastal waters and rivers. Ironically, much of this dumping is in response to stricter environmental controls on industrial wastes. These new controls raise the cost of handling wastes, and dumping is a way to avoid this burden. Even if the wastes were found, identifying their source would be nearly impossible.

Unlike factories, which release pollutants at identifiable points and are therefore known as point sources, there are many nonpoint sources where the exact source of the pollution is harder to identify and control, such as the runoff from agricultural fields. Most pollutants from these nonpoint sources are carried to the ocean by rivers.

In cities and towns, runoff from precipitation picks up paint, litter, lubricating oils, and other pollutants on the streets. Agricultural runoff usually contains pesticides, herbicides, and chemical fertilizers. Industrial runoff contains metals and organic chemicals. Nonpoint runoff is the biggest source of suspended solids and fecal coliform bacteria in U.S. waters. It also contributes more than half of the total chromium, copper, lead, iron, and zinc added to the ocean by human activities.

Petroleum is the pollutant most often associated with accidental spills in the ocean. Since World War II, the opportunities for such spills have multiplied. As energy demands have risen, increasing quantities of oil have been transported across the ocean, and more offshore drilling operations have been started. The majority of oil in the ocean comes not from dramatic tanker accidents, but from small, continuous leakages from oil refineries, industrial pipelines, offshore drilling operations, and the routine cleaning of tanker holds.

Pollutants also pass into the atmosphere through the burning of fossil fuels, the incineration of waste, or as a side effect

In what is becoming an increasingly common occurrence, a dead whale is removed from a Massachusetts beach where it became stranded during a rainstorm.

of industrial activities carried out at high temperatures. One such activity that passes large amounts of metals into the air is the roasting of limestone and shale to make cement. Winds carry these pollutants as vapors or ash particles over the ocean, where they drop with the rain into the sea.

MARINE ENVIRONMENTS AT RISK

Coastal waters and estuaries are the marine environments that have been most gravely harmed by waste-disposal activities. Several factors make these waters particularly susceptible to damage. The sunlit, nutrient-rich waters of the continental shelves are home to large quantities of fish and other marine creatures. Also, many other creatures spend the most critical, vulnerable periods of their life cycles—spawning and early growth—in these waters.

Furthermore, most wastes enter the ocean close to the coast. These waters are near communities and cities, and transporting wastes farther out to sea is very expensive. Pipelines are a primary culprit. Other important sources of waste near coastlines are rivers, though pollutants washed from rivers are usually well diluted. In some areas, nonpoint runoff or dumping poses the worst problem. Coastal areas are also at risk because pollutants are usually trapped in the sediments there or flush very slowly out to sea. Particles of sediment, and the metals and organic chemicals that bind to these particles, stick together and settle to the shallow ocean bottom. Dissolved metals come out of solution and also settle to the bottom. Currents are fairly weak in coastal areas, so pollutants are not quickly diluted.

The most endangered coastlines lie in areas of heavy urban development. The condition of the Puget Sound near Seattle, Washington, for example, is in striking contrast to the relative cleanness of most of the neighboring coastline. Lying between Seattle and the sea, the sound serves as a dump for such large amounts of toxic pollutants that it is one of the most highly contaminated areas in the country.

In comparison to coastal areas, the open ocean is generally healthy. Marine life is less concentrated in open waters, currents disperse pollutants, and the volume of wastes dumped there is currently small. The impact of human activities, however, can be seen in even the farthest reaches of the ocean. Man-made chemicals are found in plankton all over the world and in marine creatures from Arctic seals to Antarctic penguins. And plastic in

This sea gull was entangled in a plastic six-pack holder and strangled.

every conceivable form, as well as petroleum tar balls, floats thickly on the high seas.

THE IMPACT OF POLLUTANTS

When assessing the amount of pollution that enters the ocean from different sources, scientists and environmentalists look at the various impacts of these pollutants. Different types of pollutants have different effects. Also, the severity of the impact is affected by many factors, such as whether a marine creature is breeding at the time the pollutant enters the water.

Pollutants do not have to be poisonous to kill marine creatures. They are also deadly if their presence results in the loss of a key element in the biological process, such as a loss of dissolved oxygen in the water. Microorganisms in the ocean use oxygen to decompose organic material. As extra organic material is added in the form of wastes, the microorganisms become more active and use up more of the dissolved oxygen in the water. Below a critical level, there is not enough oxygen to support life. The elimination of oxygen by expanding colonies of microorganisms is known as eutrophication.

Too much of an essential element creates as much of a problem as too little. The nutrient level in coastal waters rises with the addition of runoff from fertilized farmlands and discharges from sewage plants. Up to a certain point, these increases are beneficial. Above that point, the water becomes cloudy, and sunlight, which is critical to photosynthesis, can no longer reach underwater vegetation. Plants and animals that cannot live in this new environment die. And as large numbers of particles from the

Large fleets of fishing boats using new types of nets have become so efficient that fish stocks around the world are dwindling.

runoff settle into the sediments, they smother organisms living on the bottom.

Plastics present a special danger to marine organisms. Everything from fast-food containers to automobile parts is made of plastics. Many of these products end up in the ocean, where they take centuries to decompose. Marine creatures often mistake plastic for food: turtles eat plastic bags that look like jellyfish, and birds eat tiny plastic pellets that look like fish eggs. Because the animals cannot digest or excrete the plastic, they die. Other creatures become entangled in the masses of plastic floating in the ocean.

The most dangerous pollutants in the ocean are toxic chemicals. Many of these pollutants are synthetic organic chemicals that industries have created to meet a specific need. Dichloro-diphenyl-trichloroethane (DDT), for example, was developed to kill malaria-carrying mosquitoes and agricultural pests. Polychlorinated biphenyls (PCBs) are used for many purposes, in electrical transformers and capacitators, and in hydraulic fluids, paints, and sealants.

Some organic chemicals, even though they are toxic, do not hurt marine creatures. To cause harm, a chemical has to enter an animal's body with water or food and be stored in the animal's tissues rather than be quickly excreted. This is called bio-accumulation. Even greater harm is caused to the marine en-vironment if the chemical biomagnifies. Biomagnification occurs if the level of the chemical in a creature's body increases as the animal eats other creatures that contain the chemical. Animals at the top of food chains, such as whales, dolphins, and birds, suffer the most damage from biomagnification.

Chemicals such as DDT and PCBs both bioaccumulate and biomagnify. The milk of some beluga whales in the St. Law-rence River contains PCB levels up to 3,400 times higher than the safe level for human drinking water. Products with more than 50 parts per million (ppm) of PCBs are handled as toxic substances in the United States. Yet dolphins dying off the U.S. Atlantic coast carry as much as 6,800 ppm of PCBs in their blubber. Two of the many documented impacts of DDT poisoning are the premature births of sea-lion pups and the deaths of brown pelicans eating DDT-contaminated fish.

Like organic chemicals, many metals are toxic and bioaccumulate in animal tissue. Metals either dissolve in water, where they are easily ingested by animals, or bind to sediments on the bottom. Even after being ingested, some metals pass through the digestive system and are excreted. Mercury is the only metal that biomagnifies.

Controlling emissions of a pollutant can produce a noticeable recovery in the populations of marine species. After the United States banned the use of DDT in the 1970s, the brown pelican population in California began to recover. On a global scale, though, the impact of DDT is not waning. The chemical is still widely used in the Third World and is found throughout the world's oceans.

At the top of the marine food chain, seabirds and marine mammals are vulnerable to pollution in a number of ways. A pollutant may alter a habitat or a food source. The canvasback ducks in the Chesapeake Bay, for example, lost their preferred food when pollutants killed the area's sea grasses.

Further down the food chain, fish and shellfish can be killed by pollutants that lower oxygen levels or cripple nervous systems. No one knows how many fish die in this way because most of them simply disappear into the ocean depths. At times, though, massive fish kills wash millions of dead fish up on beaches.

Smaller quantities of pollutants can be carried in animals' bodies without causing death. These pollutants threaten the health of other marine creatures and humans. One-third of the

Thousands of silver bunker fish along the Connecticut and Massachusetts coast have been dying from high water temperatures and lack of oxygen.

shellfish growing along U.S. coastlines are heavily contaminated with intestinal bacteria. Fish and other organisms living near or on the bottom accumulate the heaviest quantities of pollutants.

Fish behavior may also change after the introduction of pollutants. Fish may avoid polluted waters or become less active. The bodies of marine creatures may grow more slowly or become diseased. Fin rot, ulcers, shell erosion, tumors, and skeletal anomalies are the most noticeable of these problems.

Because of the combined stresses of overfishing and pollution, scientists estimate that the populations of all major fish species are declining around the globe.

HUMAN HEALTH

By swimming in the ocean or eating fish, people are exposed to the wastes they dump in the sea. Organic chemicals, toxic metals, and disease organisms pose the greatest danger to human health. People are also subject to the effects of biomagnification in marine food chains. The animals they eat often contain very high concentrations of a toxic chemical. In Minamata, Japan, between 1953 and 1960, an outbreak of mercury poisoning was caused by eating contaminated fish. Over 100 people died and 700 more suffered severe, permanent neurological damage.

An offshore oil rig near Mobile Bay, Alabama. Such rigs spill a significant quantity of oil into the oceans.

MANAGING OCEAN RESOURCES

Can the ocean be managed? On a physical level, the idea that people can control a mass of water covering 70% of the earth's surface is presumptuous. After all, the ocean contains 360 million cubic miles of water, while the entire population of the world would fit into only 1 cubic mile of space. Catastrophic events such as tidal waves and coastal flooding are a reminder of the massive physical forces that control these waters. Scientists have the technology to predict these events, but not to prevent them.

Managing also requires sufficient knowledge of the thing being managed. This knowledge is not currently available—either for marine or land environments. As fires raged in Yosemite National Park in the late 1980s, public officials and scientists debated whether the fires were part of the natural cycle of forest death and rebirth or an irreversible disaster. Too little is known about the ecology of forests—the interrelationships of the organisms living there and their connections with the physical environment—to know the answer. With the ocean, too, scientists are just beginning to appreciate how the impact of events and processes ripples through the environment.

The ocean's size and depth have been additional hurdles to understanding it. Studying a marine environment two miles under the surface of the ocean presents a much different and more costly technological challenge than studying a forest. Only recently have scientists begun to meet these challenges, with satellites, deep-sea drilling operations, and submersibles.

Still, human activities in the ocean can and must be better managed. The current level of use has already caused global declines in all major fish populations and in the spread of man-made chemicals throughout the ocean. The pressure on ocean resources will continue to intensify as the world's population and market demands for food, energy, and minerals escalate.

To prevent further degradation of ocean life, world communities must take three key steps to improve their manage-ment of ocean resources. First, fisheries should not be harvested according to boom-and-bust economic cycles. Such an approach threatens the food resources of the ocean because fish popu-lations are harvested with destructive technologies until they collapse. Second, the vastness of the ocean can no longer be seen as an excuse for dumping wastes. Better methods are needed to treat wastes before they are dumped into the ocean, and how and where they are dumped must be carefully regulated.

Third, the scientific community must lay a strong foun-dation for the increasing use of ocean resources with cleaner and improved technologies. Tapping certain ocean resources could answer market demands and lessen the pressure on land re-sources. If large amounts of electricity could be generated by harnessing temperature differences in the ocean, for example, less oil exploration would probably occur in national parks and reserves. At the same time, though, grave damage will be done to the ocean unless the technology is in place to exploit these resources with the least cost to the environment.

Improving the management of ocean resources will require an enormous amount of work. Research is needed, both to assess human impacts on the ocean and to explore how ocean resources can be turned to human uses. This knowledge can then be applied to developing better technologies for current activities, such as fishing, and to exploiting new resources, such as ocean thermal energy. The scientific information on new technologies will then be turned over to decision makers who govern ocean use. They can require, for example, that an industry lower its emissions of poisonous wastes or use the best available technology for a specific activity.

Laws governing the exploitation of the seas, however, must be enforceable with all the world's nations, with all their different demands and different levels of willingness and ability to help control the plunder of ocean resources. It will be necessary to create an international body with enough authority to put such laws into operation. We are now seeing the beginnings of such regulation with international treaties on the dumping of wastes and toxic and radioactive materials. When it comes to harvesting the food of the sea, however, regulation has proved much more difficult.

To lay the scientific foundation for good management of ocean resources, researchers must continue to examine marine environments and the chemistry of seawater, explore the ocean

The Greenpeace III *in waters near Polynesia. Greenpeace has been active in protesting whaling and other controversial fishing practices.*

bottom, and assess the effects of pollutants moving through the web of ocean life. These research efforts will call on specialists in a wide range of fields, including experts in computer modeling, toxicology, population dynamics, ecology, geophysics, chemistry, and oceanography.

Studying ocean environments provides an understanding of the interdependence of marine creatures. Knowing how energy flows through an ocean ecosystem is vital for predicting how pollutants will flow through that system. Understanding how a system works will also help scientists to recognize when change occurs as a result of pollution or other human pressures. The information is then available for mandating a reduction in pollution, if necessary, and for rebuilding a damaged environment.

This research can also spur improvements in the management of fisheries. Single-species management has been common and has failed. Research on entire ecosystems and their population dynamics should be used to define catch limits, which are the maximum number of each species of fish that can be harvested. For example, one reason why whales have been so poorly protected is that no one knows how many are still alive.

Research on seawater and the ocean bottom will aid ecological studies because organisms are affected by their environment as well as by their relationships to one another. This research can be used to identify and determine the feasibility of gathering new resources from the ocean. Using geological data to locate the most likely spots for mineral deposits is much quicker than trial-and-error drilling on an ocean bottom miles below.

Evaluating the impact of pollutants on the ocean is a major scientific challenge. Large numbers of synthetic and natural chemicals are poured into the ocean every day. These chemicals are degraded into a number of related chemicals or changed in form by physical and biological processes. The vastness of the ocean makes measurement and monitoring activities difficult. Because of these difficulties, scientists are often not able to prove that the introduction of a specific pollutant is causing damage to the ocean environment. Accidents are a different matter. The coating of seabirds with oil after a huge spill shows a clear cause-and-effect relationship. But most pollutants enter the ocean in small doses mixed with many other chemicals, making it difficult to determine causal factors.

In the United States, pollution is primarily managed by determining how much of a dangerous chemical can be released into the environment without causing substantial damage. This information is then used to set limits on the amount of the pollutant that can be released. Unless a chemical can be proved to cause specific damage, it cannot be regulated in this way. For decision makers to proclaim that no amount of a dangerous chemical will enter the environment is unrealistic. Instead, they must have data to show that, above a certain level, a pollutant causes unacceptable damage.

Risk assessment is a method of establishing the cause-and-effect relationship between pollutants and damage to organisms or the environment. Scientists go through four steps to determine the likelihood that a certain amount of a pollutant will cause a particular set of symptoms in organisms. For ocean environments, these steps are:

- Identifying the pollutants that cause substantial damage.
- Studying how a specific pollutant enters the ocean and moves through the marine environment.
- Identifying how much of a pollutant is taken up by animals and plants.
- Determining which health effects result from what amounts of the pollutant.

The first step is clearly needed because it is impractical to expect that all of the 65,000 chemicals used in industry world-wide can be controlled. Which ones cause the most damage to ocean environments? To decide, scientists should look at where and how rapidly a pollutant is released, how long it persists in the environment, how much it accumulates in parts of the ecosystem or in organisms, and how poisonous it is to different marine creatures.

Better monitoring techniques are needed to make these determinations. Improved methods of measuring pollutant levels in diluted seawater would be useful, especially for assessing pollutant impact on the open ocean. Also, scientists need more accurate, uniform ways to measure the amount of a chemical stored in animal tissues. The amount of a stored pollutant can vary widely between different species, different members of a single species, and different tissues within a single fish.

One approach to measuring pollution is to identify marker organisms, such as mussels and barnacles, which are known to be sensitive to specific pollutants. By watching how

A diagram of an OTEC vessel engaged in ocean thermal energy conversion. Taking advantage of differences in temperature at various depths, such experimental vessels seek to extract energy from seawater.

much of a pollutant builds up in these creatures, scientists can estimate amounts in less sensitive fish. Another approach is to concentrate efforts on the most polluted areas. Many coastlines and islands fall into this category.

The second step in assessing risk deals with what is known as fate and transport—that is, what happens to a pollutant once it enters the water. The general outline is simple, but following a pollutant through the open ocean can be complicated.

- Water currents mix and carry the pollutant away from the disposal point, such as a pipeline. Lighter materials like plastics and oil tend to float upward and heavier materials sink.
- Plants and animals take pollutants out of the water column by eating or absorbing them. As fish swim long distances, they carry the pollutants farther away.
- Pollutants sink to the bottom and are trapped in the tissues of dead fish or in their excretions. Other heavy pollutants also sink to the bottom. Most pollutants end up in the sediments.

Not all of a pollutant that is dumped into the ocean will harm marine life. Some settles into the sediments and is never eaten or absorbed. Some is eaten, but quickly excreted or broken down.

In the next step, scientists look at how much of a pollutant enters plants and animals and causes harm. This is a very important step for regulating pollutants. When regulators set limits on the amount of pollutants that can be dumped, industry costs go up, and most of these costs are passed on to the consumer. The stricter the limit, the higher the cost. Industries lobby intensely to avoid strict limits and also dump material illegally. The best way to protect the ocean is to provide reliable numbers that place the minimum necessary restrictions on industry.

Finally, scientists look at the type of damage caused by the pollutant to marine life and to the last level of the food chain—that is, human beings. At this point, they can predict the damage that will result from a specific amount of a pollutant. This information is given to the regulators who can control pollutant discharges into the ocean. The knowledge is also vital for predicting damage from large accidents and moving quickly to lessen it.

SCIENCE AND TECHNOLOGY

Science and technological development feed each other's growth. Basic science gives information to the applied sciences that is used to build and test new systems and devices. Many of these new tools are then used by scientists to gather new data. New technologies will also help lessen the impact of civilization on the ocean. Fishermen need better, less destructive ways of catching fish. Fish and shellfish can be farmed rather than hunted, but new technologies must be developed first. In terms of waste, the best option for reducing the pollution dumped into the ocean is to produce less of it. One way to do that is to recycle wastes, but recycling involves changing people's habits and working out new technologies. Those wastes that are produced must be better handled.

In this intercoastal waterway off Georgia, a speed limit has been posted for small boats to avoid injury to the endangered manatee, a large, slow-moving marine mammal.

Finally, working in the ocean to gather new resources offers amazing challenges to applied science. New materials and structures are needed that can withstand powerful physical forces such as waves, pressure, and corrosion. Better satellites and computer models of marine climate data are needed to predict weather changes more accurately and quickly. New ways are needed to find, gather, and extract the sea's resources.

For a resource to be harvested, it must meet three criteria. It must be accessible, taking into account geographic, geological, legal, political, and social factors. The technology to exploit the resource must be available. And exploitation must be economically viable—there must be a demand for the resource at a price that covers the costs of extraction.

Pressures on land resources are increasing the chances that marine resources will meet these three requirements. As long as abundant amounts of a resource are easily accessible on land, it will be cheaper than the same resource from the sea. As these land resources are depleted or become difficult to extract, ocean resources start looking more inviting.

Energy as well as physical and biological resources is available from the sea through the exploitation of waves or thermal discontinuities. Ocean space itself may be seen as a resource, as a way of isolating dangerous activities or building industrial islands out at sea. These ideas, however, are far in the future.

The most promising energy resource is ocean thermal energy conversion (OTEC). This technology uses the difference in temperature between surface waters and deeper waters to make electricity. Some scientists suggest that OTEC could provide up to 1,000 quads (quadrillion British thermal units) per year, or close to one-third of the estimated world energy demand 100 years from now.

Ocean thermal energy technologies are not yet ready to have this major an impact on world energy use. So far, they have only been proved to work at small pilot plants. For large-scale production, the industry will need floating OTEC factories at sea capable of using huge vertical pipes at least 2,500 feet long. Furthermore, the only waters where there is a great enough difference in water temperatures for OTEC to work lie in a narrow band in the tropics. Electricity will have to be transmitted from these ocean stations to the land. The resulting electricity could be used to dissociate water into hydrogen and oxygen. Hydrogen-fueled fuel cells could then be used instead of oil-, coal-, or gas-fired turbines to produce energy. Using OTEC, in other words, would eliminate the production of harmful carbon and carbon dioxide waste products, and it would lower nations' dependence on other energy sources that do produce these wastes.

Winds, waves, and tides are other possible sources of ocean energy. Using them, however, is limited to even smaller geographical areas than for OTEC. Tidal stations require large tidal ranges and a massive civil engineering commitment. Only a few really economical sites exist, such as the Severn estuary in England and the Bay of Fundy in Canada.

Some physical resources are already being extracted from the ocean in large quantities. Areas where water is in extremely short supply, such as the Middle East, depend on desalinating salt water to produce drinkable, fresh water. Water from the sea will become increasingly important as the world's supply of fresh water—for agriculture as well as for drinking—continues to dwindle.

Offshore oil drilling is also a growing industry. Most petroleum is found close to continents, where one tectonic plate plunges under another. Bottom sediments are composed of the bodies of ancient marine creatures and contain large amounts of carbon. The tremendous heat and pressure applied to these sediments as they disappear into the mantle turns them into oil. By some estimates, 40% of the world's oil will come from offshore platforms by the year 2000.

Manganese nodules, on the other hand, are only found in the deep ocean. These dark, potato-shaped lumps were first noticed in the 1960s and are thought to result from volcanic activity. Even though the nodules contain manganese, their chief value lies in other metals, such as copper, nickel, and cobalt. Like cobblestone pavements, they cover vast areas of ocean floor, sometimes extending over thousands of kilometers. Some scientists estimate that 2 to 3 billion tons of these nodules exist.

The shrimp fleet at Port Isabel, Texas. As overfishing and marine pollution reduce stocks of ocean creatures, more and more fishermen find themselves out of work.

Trying to decide how these nodules should be harvested has caused endless debate concerning the fair division of common resources. The nodules are found only in certain areas. Only a few corporations from the most industrialized countries have the resources to develop mining operations. A single such operation could cost between $900 million and $1.4 billion.

Who will receive the benefits from mining the nodules? All nations lay claim to a share of this resource. Who will pay for developing the mining technology and for the mining operations? If the industrialized nations pay but share the resource, how will they recoup their investment? Who will police the mining activities? International bodies may not have sufficient power.

Hydrothermal ore deposits, which were discovered in the 1970s, lie less deep than the manganese nodules and thus may be easier to exploit. Ocean water circulating through bottom rock layers leaches out metals from these rocks and spews them forth at hydrothermal vents. In some places, the bodies of ore may be massive. The Galápagos vents, for example, are thought to contain 8 million cubic meters of ore, mostly iron, copper, and zinc.

BIOLOGICAL RESOURCES

The boom-and-bust cycle in the exploitation of fisheries is born from the need of commercial fishermen to make a living and the desire to use as much of a common resource as possible before someone else gets it. The problem is made worse because fish populations are not evenly distributed through the world's oceans. Most are found where currents intersect coastlines and in areas where cold water wells up to the surface. Are these the world's fish, or do they belong to a specific country?

The International Convention of the Sea has answered that question by establishing exclusive economic zones (EEZs) around the coastlines of nations bordering the ocean. No other nation is supposed to fish in a country's EEZ without its consent. But this solution may only increase conflicts over fishing rights. Many of the countries with the richest EEZs do not have the technology or the infrastructure to manage them well. Overfishing is likely to continue in these areas. Also, since countries can lease fishing rights within their EEZs, tremendous pressure may be exerted on poor countries to lease these rich fishing grounds, thereby losing their benefits. Competition will be particularly intense in Asian countries, where fish make up 55% of the protein consumed.

Mariculture, or sea farming, is an important option for increasing fish and shellfish yield and reducing pressure on wild stocks. Sea farmers raise fingerlings, larvae, or small plants in sheltered areas of the ocean, enclosed ponds, submerged cages, or lagoons until they are fully grown and ready for market.

Mariculture requires considerable technological improvement before it becomes widely economical. Even though it has been used in Asia for centuries, these operations have usually been quite small. Seeding the operation, for example, is difficult. Baby fish and shellfish are difficult to obtain in the wild, and many species will not breed in captivity. Mariculture works best when technologies are adapted to local cultures, and few potential sea farmers have the knowledge needed.

If these problems can be overcome, however, mariculture offers many advantages. It provides employment in underde-

A brown pelican killed by oil contamination near Corpus Christi, Texas.

veloped countries, and fish are a highly profitable kind of protein to cultivate. Fish convert their food into flesh more efficiently than does livestock, so the sea farmer gathers more pounds of food for his or her labor. Seaweed is another excellent product for the sea farmer. It can be used for food, animal feed, or fertilizer.

Terrestrial plants and animals have long been important sources for new medicines and drugs. Marine organisms have a similarly rich potential. Hormones, antibiotics, and other substances have already been isolated from animals, bacteria, algae, and fungi. Scientists are extremely interested in marine poisons, such as the neurotoxin from the blowfish, or puffer. One of these toxins has worked well as a local anesthetic in surgery. Another toxin secreted from a marine worm seems to be an excellent insecticide. To manage the ocean, a value must be placed on it. What is the dollar value of people's activities around the ocean? What is the dollar value of a healthy marine environment? Decision makers use this information to develop laws and regulations for balancing the competing needs of different interest groups and nations.

Calculating the dollar value of people's activities around the ocean is relatively easy. In the United States, for example, over 13 million adults used Florida beaches in 1984, leading to $4.6 billion in beach-related sales. Almost 12 million Americans fish recreationally and spend approximately $2.4 billion on food, lodging, transportation, equipment, and licenses. About 231,000 commercial fishermen were employed in the U.S. in 1984. Total commercial landings of fish and shellfish in 1985 were worth $2.3 billion at dockside and several times greater at the retail level.

When the population of a fish collapses because of overfishing, or a popular beach is closed because of pollution, beach communities are faced with a financial loss. No one spends money at the beach. Fishermen are out of work. These quantifiable costs can be used to force change.

Another kind of value—the value of a pristine environment—can be as hard to estimate for the oceans as it is for a stand of ancient redwoods. Some people take great joy in walking along a beach as the sun rises or in watching ocean creatures. Others simply feel that it is wrong to treat the natural world as if its only reason for being is to meet people's needs and pleasures. Attitudes such as these make people value the undisturbed ocean highly.

Aesthetic reactions, however, are not enough to protect a single fish. Many people are more concerned about keeping local industries viable and making profits. To be heard in the clamor of competing interests, environmentalists must quantify the value they place on the oceans. One way to do this is to point to the costs communities and nations will eventually pay for pollution and overfishing. There are the local costs of lost beach revenues and jobs, but the global effects of ocean damage provide an even more powerful argument. An increasing number of scientists and members of the general public are realizing that activities in the oceans can harm the climate as much as spewing carbon dioxide–laden smoke into the air.

A key global-level effect of pollution is the loss of biodiversity. Biodiversity refers to the number of different living species and the diversity of genetic information they carry. Without genetic diversity, entire populations are less able to adapt to change. The common reasons given for protecting biodiversity are human-centered, such as maintaining sources of food, new drugs, and genetic stock for breeding. Much more important is the ability of a healthy, diverse biosphere to support the earth's geochemical cycles.

INTERNATIONAL AGREEMENTS AND CONVENTIONS

Many attempts have been made to establish a comprehensive law governing the common waters of the ocean. The most recent of these efforts is the United Nations Conference on the Law of the Sea, which began in 1970 with a U.N. resolution declaring the oceans a "common heritage of mankind" in need of both protection and study. The Convention of the Sea was completed in 1982 but has been ratified by only 35 nations, not including the United States.

Even though the signatures of 60 nations are needed for the convention to go into effect, many nations are already claiming the 200-mile exclusive economic zones (EEZs) established by the convention off their shores. EEZs move 90% of the ocean's fish, as well as most of the known deposits of oil and gas, into national jurisdictions. According to some observers, this may not be the best way to resolve national conflicts over fishing rights, but it may be the only realistic way.

The EEZ concept leaves many issues unresolved. For example, the United States has passed legislation declaring that salmon spawned in U.S. waters are American, no matter where they wander. Who owns the rich resources off Antarctica? Why should one nation make an effort to protect a fish population if another nation is going to destroy it once the fish move into a different part of the ocean?

Four other international conventions and programs need to be mentioned. First is the Convention on the Prevention of Marine Pollution by Dumping of Wastes and Other Matter, or the London Dumping Convention (LDC). The LDC has been ratified by 65 nations, including the United States. It identifies a "black list" of hazardous materials that countries are prohibited from dumping into the sea, such as radioactive materials and heavy metals like mercury. The LDC's "gray list" contains materials that may be dumped with special permits. Even though dumping is not the leading cause of pollution, the LDC is an important step.

The International Convention for the Prevention of Pollution from Ships (MARPOL) controls pollution from ocean-going vessels. The MARPOL regulations are divided into five parts, three of which the United States has ratified. The first part covers oil pollution from ships, most of which involves small-scale discharges from normal operations and vessel cleaning. Since MARPOL was put in place, a noticeable decrease in numbers of oil-covered animals has occurred.

The United Nations Environment Program (UNEP) is the most important international institution devoted to the protection of the environment in general and to the marine environment in particular. Its regional seas program is intended to develop local arrangements for controlling pollution and managing marine resources. This program encompasses 10 regional seas with over 120 nations participating.

Finally, the International Whaling Commission (IWC) is an example of an international marine management effort that has failed. The IWC, with 38 member nations, was established in 1946 to regulate the hunting of whales. It did not prevent the continued decimation of all major whale populations. Nor did it prevent nations such as Japan, Norway, and the Soviet Union from ignoring its moratorium on whaling, passed in 1986. The IWC is powerless.

Besides ratifying and enforcing international conventions and programs, nations are responsible for protecting the marine resources near their own coasts. To do so, they need a well-balanced, integrated set of laws covering marine environments and resources. Instead, the United States has a hodgepodge of laws that overlap one another and are enforced by different authorities. An integrated approach and stricter regulations must be put in place to implement these laws, and agencies must be given the power to enforce the regulations. One increasingly popular approach to stricter regulation is to make polluters pay for their activities. If the penalty is great enough, polluters may be encouraged to reduce pollution at the source.

The alarming decline of marine ecosystems suggests that regulations, however well enforced, will not be enough to protect the oceans. Governments must also provide economic and scientific support for industries and farming operations that are exploring a different approach to development. For example, new production methods could be designed that do not produce toxic wastes, and agricultural methods that do not rely on chemical fertilizers and pesticides must be encouraged.

Another challenge for developed nations is to persuade less developed nations not to follow in their footsteps. Less developed nations see no reason why the wealthy nations should adopt a high, moral tone about the environment when they gathered their wealth by ravaging the environment and have still not mended their ways. The developed nations need to set a better example and to offer economic incentives to developing nations to try a different approach. Many poor people in developing countries are aware that cutting down trees and overharvesting the ocean will destroy their environment, but they see no other way to feed their families. They need help in developing alternative technologies and sustainable methods of feeding themselves.

INTEGRATED RESOURCE MANAGEMENT

To protect marine resources, national and local governments must undertake a multifaceted approach. First, they must establish national standards for the use and exploitation of coastlines. Second, they should set up enforceable regional management plans. Such plans will control all the competing demands for coastal resources and space. Third, and perhaps most important, local governments must support programs in schools that describe the ocean as a vital living system needing protection. An attitude can be fostered in communities that protecting the ocean is good business and good sense.

One of the most popular ways for nations to protect marine resources is to set aside areas for reserves, or marine parks. These areas, such as the Great Barrier Reef in Australia, often attract large numbers of tourists. But because of the fluid nature of the environment, marine parks are difficult to protect. Fish swim in and out of the park, and pollution drifts in from neighboring areas. Park management is often not equipped to protect the resources in its care. At Coco Island, Costa Rica, for example, park rangers have one small, underpowered skiff with which they are supposed to catch dozens of full-sized boats fishing for shark.

Another problem is the fact that scientists simply do not know enough about ocean environments to manage them. This limitation was highlighted recently in Australia, when the crown-of-thorns starfish started decimating wide swaths of coral reef. Large sums of money were spent to study the starfish, but park management still does not know if the jump in the starfish population was due to human interference or part of the natural cycle of reef life.

Another approach to marine protection is grass-roots activism. Currently, the most active group in the field is Greenpeace, which sends boats to block whalers and to free dolphins and birds from fishing nets. People fight the hardest to protect their own backyard. By working to protect the seas and by physically obstructing harmful activities, Greenpeace has made the ocean its own backyard. It is time that more people thought that way.

APPENDIX: FOR MORE INFORMATION

Environmental Organizations

Center for Marine Conservation
1235 DeSales Street NW
Washington, DC 20036
(202) 429-5609

Climatic Institute
316 Pennsylvania Avenue SE
Washington, DC 20003
(202) 547-0104

Cousteau Society
930 West 21st Street
Norfolk, VA 23517
(804) 627-1144

Earth Island Institute
300 Broadway, Suite 28
San Francisco, CA 94133
(415) 788-7324

Environmental Defense Fund
257 Park Avenue South
New York, NY 10010
(212) 505-2100

Friends of the Earth
Take Back the Coast!
Campaign
218 D Street SE
Washington, DC 20003
(202) 544-2600

Greenpeace
1436 U Street NW
Washington, DC 20009
(202) 462-1177

League of Conservation
Voters
1150 Connecticut Street NW
Washington, DC 20036
(202) 785-8683

National Audubon Society
950 Third Avenue
New York, NY 10022
(212) 832-3200

National Wildlife Federation
1400 16th Street NW
Washington, DC 20036
(202) 797-6800

Natural Resources Defense
 Council
40 West 20th Street
New York, NY 10011
(212) 727-2700

Sierra Club
730 Polk Street
San Francisco, CA 94109
(415) 776-2211

Valdez Principles Coalition for
 Environmentally Responsible
 Economies
711 Atlantic Avenue, Fifth Floor
Boston, MA 02111
(617) 451-0927

Water Pollution Control
 Federation
601 Wythe Street
Alexandria, VA 22314
(703) 684-2400

Government Agencies

Environmental Protection
 Agency
401 M Street SW
Washington, DC 20460
(202) 382-2090

National Park Service
Department of the Interior
P. O. Box 37127
Washington, DC 20013
(202) 208-4747

U.S. Fish and Wildlife
 Service
Department of the Interior
1849 C Street NW
Washington, DC 20240
(202) 208-5634

FURTHER READING

Attenborough, David. *Life on Earth.* Boston: Little Brown, 1979.

Barton, Robert. *The Oceans.* New York: Facts on File, 1980.

Broecker, Wallace S., and George H. Denton. "What Drives Glacial Cycles?" *Scientific American,* 262(1):48. 1990.

Clark, Eugenie. *The Lady and the Sharks.* New York: Harper and Row, 1969.

Cousteau, J., and staff of the Cousteau Society. *The Cousteau Almanac.* New York: Doubleday, 1981.

Davis, Lloyd Spencer. "Penguin Weighting Game," *Natural History,* January 1991.

Durrell, Lee. *State of the Ark.* New York: Doubleday, 1986.

Earle, Sylvia A., and Al Giddings. *Exploring the Deep Frontier— The Adventure of Man in the Sea.* Washington, DC: National Geographic Society, 1980.

Harrison, Richard, and M. M. Bryden. *Whales, Dolphins, and Porpoises.* New York: Facts on File, 1988.

Kaufman, Les, and Kenneth Mallory, eds. *The Last Extinction.* Cambridge: MIT Press, 1986.

Levine, Joseph. *Undersea Life.* New York: Stewart, Tabori & Chang. 1985.

Naveen, Ron, et al. *Wild Ice—Antarctic Journeys.* Washington, D.C.: Smithsonian Institution Press, 1970.

Thorne-Miller, Boyce, and John Catena. *The Living Ocean: Understanding and Protecting Marine Biodiversity.* Washington, DC: Island Press, 1991.

Vincent, Amanda. "A Seahorse Father Makes a Good Mother," *Natural History,* December 1990, p. 34.

White, Robert M. "The Great Climate Debate," *Scientific American* 263(1): 36. 1990.

GLOSSARY

algae   Simple photosynthetic plants; they may be unicellular or
multicellular, but they do not have specialized organs such as
leaves, stems, and roots.

atmosphere of pressure   A unit of measurement, one atmosphere of
pressure is the pressure of the air on the earth's surface at sea level;
the pressure of seawater increases by one atmosphere for every 33
feet of depth.

benthic   Of or having to do with the bottom of the ocean.

bioaccumulation   The accumulation of toxic chemicals in the tissues of
living organisms.

bioluminescence   The phosphorescent light created by living organisms,
usually to attract prey or mates.

biomagnification   An increase in the concentration of a toxic
chemical with each new link in the food chain, resulting in higher
concentrations in the tissues of animals (such as dolphins, whales,
seabirds, and humans) at the top of a food chain.

biosphere   That part of the earth that supports life.

continental shelf   The shallow platform that slopes gradually out from a
continent to a depth of about 100 fathoms and ends in an abrupt
descent to deeper water.

continental slope   The slope that extends downward from the outer edge
of the continental shelf to the ocean floor.

Coriolis factor   A force that affects any body moving on a rotating
surface, acting at right angles to the body's direction of movement;
due to the earth's rotation, the Coriolis force causes objects to veer

to the right in the Northern Hemisphere and to the left in the Southern Hemisphere.

ecosystem   A biological community and its physical environment.

electromagnetic radiation   Energy emitted in the form of electromagnetic waves, from very long, low-frequency radio waves, through infrared and light waves, to the very short, high-frequency cosmic rays and X rays.

El Niño   A warm ocean current that appears off the coast of South America in December and prevents cold, nutrient-rich water from upwelling along the coast, causing starvation among birds and fish; El Niño is a global phenomenon, and during intense El Niños weather changes occur from Australia to California.

infrared rays   The invisible part of the electromagnetic spectrum, including rays with wavelengths longer than those of visible red light but shorter than microwaves.

magma chamber   An enclosed space containing molten material beneath the earth's crust.

oceanic crust   The solid outer layer of the earth lying under the ocean and resting on the mantle.

ooze   The soft mud or slime found on the ocean floor that is formed from millions of shells and skeletons from tiny plants and animals; oozes eventually harden into rock, such as limestone.

photosynthesis   The process by which plants make carbohydrates by combining carbon dioxide and water in the presence of chlorophyll and light, and release oxygen as a by-product.

phytoplankton   Small plants or plantlike organisms, usually algae, that create energy compounds through photosynthesis.

plankton   The small organisms that float or drift in the water, especially at or near the surface; plankton include small crustaceans, algae, and protozoans, and serve as an important source of food for larger animals, such as fish.

plate tectonics The theory that the earth's crust is divided into a series of vast, platelike parts that move or drift as distinct masses.

pollution The contamination of a natural ecosystem by wastes from human activities.

remote sensing The acquisition of physical data about an object without touching or contacting it by recording and analyzing electromagnetic radiation.

subduction zone The area where one crustal plate sinks or is pushed under part of another.

submersible A vessel capable of operating or remaining underwater.

species diversity The number of species in a region.

zooplankton Animal plankton, including protozoans, sea anemones, corals, and jellyfishes.

INDEX

London Dumping Convention. *See*
Convention on the Prevention
of Marine Pollution by
Dumping of Wastes and Other
Matter

Malaria, 70
Manganese nodules, 87, 88
Mariculture, 89, 91
Marine parks, 96–97
Mediterranean Sea, 30
Mercury, 71, 73, 94
Miami, 35
Middle East, 30, 86
Mid-Ocean Ridge, 27–28, 29, 43,
  49
Minamata, Japan, 73
Mississippi River, 26
Molten rock, 14
Morocco, 30
Mosquitoes, 70
Mount Everest, 25
Mussels, 50, 81

Niagara Falls, 30
Nickel, 87
Nitrates, 53
Nitrogen, 39
North America, 26, 28, 31,
  37
Northern Europe, 14
Northern Hemisphere, 19, 35
Norway, 95
Notothenioids, 44, 45–46

Ocean
  and air currents, 14, 18, 19
  in ancient times, 21, 30, 31
  animal life, 13, 14, 16, 38, 39,
    43, 44–51, 56, 59, 60,
    61–62, 66, 70, 71, 72, 76,
    83, 89, 91
  birth, 26
  canyons, 25
  carbon dioxide, 39–40
  climate, 14, 16, 18, 21, 22,
    31, 40
  crust, 14, 28
  deep currents, 20, 34, 35
  explorers, 14, 15
  farming, 89, 91
  floor, 25, 26–27, 28
  food chain, 14, 38, 40, 44,
    50, 62
  gases, 14, 21
  glacial periods, 36–37
  gods, 13
  heat, 14, 18, 21, 23, 32, 33
  historical view, 13
  human effects on, 23, 60–61,
    63, 64,
  human management, 75
  and light, 32
  as "memory" of atmosphere,
    33
  movement, 14
  movement of continents, 17,
    21, 37
  nutrients, 26, 37, 49, 50, 51,
    52, 68–69
  plant life, 15–16, 27, 32–33,
    37–38, 40
  pollution, 14, 34, 40, 59, 63
  radiation of light, 18
  resources, 85
  role in earth's climate, 14
  salt, 20, 21
  sediments, 17, 23, 29, 39, 40,
    41
  as seen from satellites, 14

PICTURE CREDITS

Conversion Table

(From U.S./English system units to metric system units)

Length

1 inch = 2.54 centimeters
1 foot = 0.305 meters
1 yard = 0.91 meters
1 statute mile = 1.6 kilometers (km.)

Area

1 square yard = 0.84 square meters
1 acre = 0.405 hectares
1 square mile = 2.59 square km.

Liquid Measure

1 fluid ounce = 0.03 liters
1 pint (U.S.) = 0.47 liters
1 quart (U.S.) = 0.95 liters
1 gallon (U.S.) = 3.78 liters

Weight and Mass

1 ounce = 28.35 grams
1 pound = 0.45 kilograms
1 ton = 0.91 metric tons

Temperature

1 degree Fahrenheit = 0.56 degrees Celsius or centigrade, but to convert from actual Fahrenheit scale measurements to Celsius, subtract 32 from the Fahrenheit reading, multiply the result by 5, and then divide by 9. For example, to convert 212° F to Celsius:

$$212 - 32 = 180 \times 5 = 900 \div 9 = 100° C$$

ABOUT THE AUTHOR

ELIZABETH COLLINS is a Massachusetts-based writer who has written extensively on science topics, including articles for *Scientific American, Nature, Earthwatch,* and *Health.* She has a B.A. in English from Princeton University, an M.A.T. in English from Vanderbilt University, and an M.S. in science journalism from Boston University. When she is not scuba diving, Ms. Collins is a senior writer for Eastern Research Group, Inc., an environmental research organization in Arlington, Massachusetts.

ABOUT THE EDITOR

RUSSELL E. TRAIN, currently chairman of the board of directors of the World Wildlife Fund and The Conservation Foundation, has had a long and distinguished career of government service under three presidents. In 1957 President Eisenhower appointed him a judge of the United States Tax Court. He served Lyndon Johnson on the National Water Commission. Under Richard Nixon he became under secretary of the Interior and, in 1970, first chairman of the Council on Environmental Quality. From 1973 to 1977 he served as administrator of the Environmental Protection Agency. Train is also a trustee or director of the African Wildlife Foundation; the Alliance to Save Energy; the American Conservation Association; Citizens for Ocean Law; Clean Sites, Inc.; the Elizabeth Haub Foundation; the King Mahendra Trust for Nature Conservation (Nepal); Resources for the Future; the Rockefeller Brothers Fund; the Scientists' Institute for Public Information; the World Resources Institute; and Union Carbide and Applied Energy Services, Inc. Train is a graduate of Princeton and Columbia Universities, a veteran of World War II, and currently resides in the District of Columbia.